WITH A SONG IN MY HEART

Brennan had let Elle get too close to him tonight. He couldn't handle that. He was going to have to put some distance between the two of them. Thank God he was leaving on a business trip.

He did a lot of thinking during the night hours, the image of Elle burning into his mind. There were so many things he wanted to say to her, but a lifetime of restraint held him back.

Elle was asleep when he returned to the master bedroom. As quietly as he could manage, Brennan undressed and eased into bed. She turned on her side, her back to him. He moved closer, throwing his arm across her waist.

Brennan closed his eyes as he relished the feel of Elle's body. He needed her warmth to melt the ice around his heart. Only she could never know.

BOOK YOUR PLACE ON OUR WEBSITE AND MAKE THE ARABESQUE ROMANCE CONNECTION!

We've created a customized website just for our very special Arabesque readers, where you can get the inside scoop on everything that's going on with Arabesque romance novels.

When you come online, you'll have the exciting opportunity to:

- View covers of upcoming books

- Learn about our future publishing schedule (listed by publication month and author)

- Find out when your favorite authors will be visiting a city near you

- Search for and order backlist books

- Check out author bios and background information

- Send e-mail to your favorite authors

- Join us in weekly chats with authors, readers and other guests

- Get writing guidelines

- AND MUCH MORE!

Visit our website at
http://www.arabesquebooks.com

WITH A SONG IN MY HEART

Jacquelin Thomas

BET Publications, LLC
http://www.bet.com

ARABESQUE BOOKS are published by

BET Publications, LLC
c/o BET BOOKS
One BET Plaza
1900 W Place NE
Washington, DC 20018-1211

All Kensington Titles, Imprints, and Distributed Lines are available at special quantity discounts for bulk purchases for sales promotions, premiums, fund-raising, and educational or institutional use. Special book excerpts or customized printings can also be created to fit specific needs. For details, write or phone the office of the Kensington special sales manager: Kensington Publishing Corp., 850 Third Avenue, New York, NY 10022, attn: Special Sales Department, Phone: 1-800-221-2647.

First Printing: December 2001
10 9 8 7 6 5 4 3 2 1

Printed in the United States of America

This book is dedicated to Patricia Worthington and Sharonlyn Campbell—two wonderful women whose delightful charm, wisdom, and friendship epitomize the very essence of true G.R.I.T.S. (Girls Raised in the South).

ACKNOWLEDGMENTS

First and foremost, I have to thank God for giving me this talent and for allowing me to live out my dream.

I have to thank my family, as always. To my best friend and husband, Bernard: I really appreciate you and all that you've done. Thanks for making sure the children have what they need and for all those dinners you've prepared so that I can stay on deadline. To my daughter Lauren: Thanks for taking care of your little brother and for all the delicious meals you've cooked, freeing me up to write. I appreciate you, baby girl. To my daughter Bevin (Nikki): You're a grown woman now and on your own, but know that I love you dearly and will always be there for you.

To the Wake County Human Services Child Care Division: You all are truly amazing women. It's been such a pleasure working with everyone. Thank you all for not only welcoming me, but also supporting me in my writing. Most of all, thanks for working around my writing schedule.

Prologue

The room hadn't been quiet long as the morning sun climbed higher into the heavens. Tangled in a mass of damp sheets, Brennan lay on his side, gazing at the sleeping woman beside him. He couldn't seem to tear his eyes away. To him, Elle Ransom was the most beautiful woman he'd ever seen. Watching her sleep like this . . . his emotions defied words. He'd never felt his heart pound so hard from nothing more than just looking at a woman.

Elle groggily pursued the warmth of his nearness, fitting her naked body to the planes and angles of his. Still sleeping, she insinuated her leg between his and curved her arm around his waist.

Brennan's thoughts centered on the first time he ever laid eyes on Elle. She had been sitting inside her office at Jupiter Records, holding her pen in the manner of a cigarette. She'd seemed to be weighed down in her thoughts, never noticing that she was being watched. A few minutes later, she'd laid the pen down, exhaled softly, and leaned forward over her desk. That's when she'd noticed him. . . .

Elle gave a soft moan, drawing him back to the present. Her peaceful expression brought a tender smile to Brennan's lips. He leaned down and gave her a delicate kiss on her forehead.

He kissed her again. This time she mumbled something unintelligible. Lightly he fingered a loose tendril of hair on her cheek. "What did you say, sleeping beauty?" he questioned, his voice a whisper.

"I love you," Elle murmured in her sleep.

Brennan hurtled back to earth as reality struck. He'd known for months about her crush on him and had been flattered. That was part of the reason he'd asked her out in the first place. But that wasn't the whole of it. Sure, Brennan was attracted to Elle. He even cared for her—more than he dared admit even to himself—but love was not a part of the arrangement. He had not signed on for that.

Somewhere along the way, things had changed between them, and Brennan wasn't happy about it. In truth, he was scared. He stole a peek at Elle and swallowed with difficulty. She was still sleeping peacefully, a tiny smile on her face. He sighed in sadness because he knew what would have to be done. They had reached the point where their relationship had to be defined.

Slipping out of bed, Brennan padded naked into the bathroom. When he came out a short time later, he was fully dressed. Brennan gazed at Elle as if he were photographing her. He felt an instant's squeezing hurt and tried to swallow the lump that lingered in his throat. Feeling older than his thirty-eight years, he strode quietly out of the bedroom.

Pain, sharp and sickening in its intensity, flowed

through him. He knew that it would take time to forget Elle's sweet smile, the sound of her soft laughter, and the sultry look she always gave him. Brennan would never forget her touch or the way her body felt beneath his. . . .

He shook off the thoughts and crept to the door. A few minutes later he was in his car, driving away from the house and out of Elle's life, while ignoring the throbbing ache in his heart. Love had no place in his life. He had lived much too long without it.

Chapter One

"Rhyan Elle Ransom, do you take Brennan Edward Cunningham III as your husband . . ."

Suddenly a shrill noise resounded in the room. Jolted out of a beautiful dream, Elle shot up in bed and reached out to turn off the screaming alarm clock. Pressing her hands to her stomach, she whispered, "It was just a dream. Just a dream, little one."

As her heartbeat gradually returned to normal, Elle's eyes bounced around the room, straying briefly to the clock resting on a dark oak nightstand. Eight-fifteen. She swiped at her face before slipping out of bed.

On her way to the bathroom, Elle stopped briefly to finger the silver-colored bridesmaid dress hanging from her closet door. Today her brother was getting married. Although she was genuinely happy for Nyle, it was hard to watch two people so obviously in love, when one's own heart was in shreds. Nyle and Chandra had chosen to get married on Valentine's Day, and it struck a painful chord within her. Cupid had taken his best shot and missed big-time where she was concerned.

Elle was single, twenty-five years old, and pregnant. Financially, she was doing okay. For the most part, she had no regrets over her decision to keep her pregnancy a secret from Brennan. Well, almost. Especially after the way he'd treated her. Two months ago, he'd walked out of her life and moved to France. She hadn't heard from him since.

Elle could have very easily gotten a message to him—especially since Brennan and her boss, Malcolm Turner, were best friends. But she opted to raise her baby alone.

Over her musings, Elle heard footsteps in the hallway, then a knock on her door.

"Come in," she called out cheerfully, knowing instinctively that it was her twin.

Nyle stuck his head inside the room. "Morning, sis. How're you feeling?"

Elle managed a smile. "I'm fine."

He stepped all the way into the room. "No morning sickness?"

Shaking her head no, she answered, "I'm fine, Nyle. You don't have to worry. I won't be passing out at your wedding."

He laughed. "That's not what I'm worried about. I just wanted to make sure you're doing okay."

She gazed into the dark brown eyes that were identical to her own. "I'm not the one who was out late at a bachelor party." Folding her arms across her chest, Elle inquired, "What time did you finally come home?"

"Around three, I think."

"Maybe we should be concerned about *you* passing out during the ceremony. Don't pull a Preston on us."

Elle fondly recalled the wedding of their oldest brother and the way he'd fainted just before he'd said his vows.

Nyle broke into laughter over the memory. "Preston just dropped to the floor like a rock. Man, that was something. I couldn't believe it."

The siblings shared another round of laughter.

Giving Nyle a light shove, she ordered, "Now go on and get out of my room so I can take a shower. When I'm done, I'll come down and make you some breakfast. I don't want you getting married on an empty stomach."

He gave her a strange look.

"What? Why are you looking at me like that?"

"We're all gathering at La Maison for brunch. Don't you remember?"

Elle searched her memory. "No. When did that come about?"

"Kaitlin suggested it the other night at the rehearsal dinner." Nyle paused for a second. "You left early, though. She must have mentioned it after you left."

"Well, it works for me. I'm tired of cooking for you anyway," she teased.

"After today, you won't have to worry about it."

Elle was suddenly serious. "I'm going to miss having you as a roommate." She hugged him, holding him tight.

"Will you be okay? Handling the rent by yourself, I mean."

Elle nodded. "Jillian and John offered to cover your half of the rent. Mama, of course, suggested that I just move back home." She gave a small laugh. "I told all of them that I'll be fine. I've built up a small savings and I make a pretty good salary, so I can handle the rent by myself. I'm even thinking of buying the house from Jillian."

Nyle lifted her chin with his hand. "If you need my help with anything, I'm here for you, Elle. I'll even be your labor coach."

With a wave of her hand, Elle dismissed his comment. "We're twins and all, but there are some things I'd like to keep to myself, if you know what I mean."

He grinned. "When those labor pains hit you, I'll bet you won't care how much of you I see. Besides, I'd be at your head."

Laughing, Elle shook her head. "That's all right. I'll ask Jillian, Carrie, or Kaitlin. Ivy and Allura would get on my nerves."

Nyle headed to the door. "I'll leave you to your shower."

"I'm really happy for you. I want you to know that."

He tossed her a look over his shoulder. "I love you, too, sis."

The candlelight wedding ceremony was an elegant affair, filled with celebrities and other notables among the guests. Nothing less for the daughter of Los Angeles Mayor Willard Davis.

In keeping with the Valentine's Day theme, the florist used red anemones, red roses, and red berries, with greenery mixed in to soften the look of the arrangement, placed in silver containers. Silver votives were wrapped in red organza, and rose petals were scattered on the tablecloths.

Butter and cheeses had been cut into heart shapes. Nyle and Chandra had even ordered candy hearts that said JUST MARRIED. For favors, guests were given candy-filled crystal heart-shaped boxes with the bride's and groom's names and wedding date engraved.

"I guess you could say this is definitely the wedding to end all weddings," Allura whispered. She gave a discreet point of her finger at a nearby cameraman. "He's from *Jet* magazine."

Elle nodded but did not comment. She swiftly scanned the room, stopping nowhere in particular. From the moment she'd stepped into the church, Elle had experienced a series of strange sensations. Even now the hair on the back of her neck stood up, and her stomach felt funny. Placing a hand on her right arm, Elle gazed around the room once more.

She had no idea what or who she was looking for until her eyes met those of a man standing a few feet away. He looked at her with a slightly lifted brow, and his gaze raked her with a thoroughness that made her waver between anger and excitement.

He stood six feet three inches tall, his shoulders broad and muscular. Brennan was wearing a tuxedo that she knew had been tailored just for him. He was still as handsome as ever. Her eyes stayed with him as he strode purposefully toward her.

No, her inner voice cried. *Don't come over here. I'm not ready to see you. I can't handle this right now.*

Despite all the anger she felt, Elle couldn't stop her heart from wanting him. She didn't even know how to try. This man had broken her heart just two months ago, and now here she was—feeling weak at the knees over seeing him.

"Miss Ransom, you're looking as beautiful as ever," he said, his voice deep and rich.

"Hello, Brennan." Elle could feel her sister giving him a hostile once-over. Talking quickly, she introduced them.

"I'm so glad to finally meet you, Brennan." Allura

spoke the words, yet Elle doubted she really meant them. None of her siblings were pleased with the fact that Brennan had seduced her, then abruptly left for Europe without a word. Truth be told, she didn't like it much, either.

"Me, too."

His response seemed automatic and programmed.

Elle was finding it hard to believe Brennan was actually standing right in front of her. It had been two months since she'd last seen him, but he'd approached her as if he'd seen her yesterday. She swallowed hard, trying not to think about that day back in December. That had been one of the most painful moments of her life.

Elle flicked Allura a glance that caused her to excuse herself. Turning her attention to Brennan, Elle held her tongue. She intended to hear him out. She would at least give him the benefit of the doubt.

Brennan's gaze met hers. "So, Chandra married your brother. I had no idea."

"Nyle and I are twins," Elle blurted out. Embarrassment flooded her face. That was not at all what she had intended to say.

"I remember your telling me you had a twin."

They talked for a few minutes more about the Davis family.

It soon became increasingly clear that Brennan had no intention of giving her any explanation for his past actions. Elle felt a surge of anger, but controlled it with effort. "I'm kind of surprised to see you here. When did you return from Europe?"

By Brennan's apparently amused reaction, he had been anticipating this question.

"Just a few days ago. I flew back for the wedding."

This infuriated her more. "*I see*," she stated coolly. His response managed to wound Elle. Determined not to let Brennan know how much it hurt, she switched back to the subject of the wedding. "It was a beautiful ceremony, don't you think?"

He shrugged in nonchalance. "It was a good performance. That's all weddings are, you know."

Elle considered Brennan's comment odd, but she stayed silent. His next words cut into her thoughts. "Elle, tell me something. Just how many brothers and sisters do you have?"

Puzzled by his question, she replied, "I have four sisters and five brothers, why?"

"They all seem to have their eyes on us. At least I'm assuming these people are your relatives. You all favor one another."

She glanced around, following his gaze. Turning back to face him, Elle acknowledged, "They're my family. We're all very close."

"Are they always this nosy?"

Folding her arms across her chest, Elle frowned. "Excuse me?"

"Well, they do seem really interested in what's going on between us."

Giving a slight shrug, she replied, "They care about me. Do *you* have a problem with that?"

Brennan gave a soft chuckle. "You don't have to sound so defensive. I don't care about them. Your brothers certainly don't scare me."

"They shouldn't," she replied flippantly. "It's the Ransom women you should worry about." Having said that, Elle turned on her heel and walked off. She was beginning to find Brennan Cunningham III irritating.

He followed her. Reaching out, Brennan grabbed her hand and said, "I didn't mean to upset you. I'm sorry."

Looking up into his face, Elle just stared at him. She fought the urge to kiss him or to lose herself in his gaze.

He gave her one of his devastating smiles. "Forgive me?"

Each time he flashed her one of those smiles, Elle's body warmed in response. Brennan's sexy full lips, his smooth dark chocolate skin, and his mahogany eyes all together presented a subtle handsomeness. She had always been attracted to bald men, and it didn't matter that he was thirteen years older than she.

Elle gave a slight wave of dismissal. "There's nothing to forgive, Brennan." Bile rose from her stomach and threatened to choke her. With grim determination, she forced it back down. Elle placed a hand on her stomach but quickly removed it.

Brennan was eyeing her, his gaze full of questions.

Hoping to sidetrack any suspicions he might be having, Elle said, "Maybe I should be the one apologizing. I'm really not feeling too well right now, and when I don't feel good I get irritable."

Brennan's expression was instantly one of concern. "Would you like to sit down?" He had not released his hold on her arm.

"Yes, if you don't mind." Elle prayed the sudden onslaught of nausea would soon dissipate. She was grateful to have Brennan to lean on for the moment.

He led Elle over to an empty table, where he pulled out a chair for her. When she was seated, Brennan joined her, quickly signaling to a waiter.

"Could you please get Miss Ransom a glass of water?"

The waiter nodded. "I'll be back shortly."

Elle hadn't been seated long before she began to

experience the return of the strange sensations she'd felt earlier. The hair on the back of her neck prickled and her stomach was in knots. She glanced over to her right and found a woman staring at her. Elle had no idea who she was, but she smiled nonetheless. The woman did not return her smile, only continued to stare.

"That's my mother," Brennan announced.

Elle looked back at him. "She doesn't look too happy right now." Mrs. Cunningham had given her the feeling that she strongly disapproved of Brennan talking to her. But why? "Does she have a problem with you talking to me?"

Brennan gave a slight shrug of nonchalance. "It doesn't matter. I'm a grown man."

The waiter returned with a fresh pitcher of ice water. He poured the cold liquid into a glass and handed it to Elle.

She thanked him and took a sip, then another, and waited for her stomach to settle down. She prayed she wouldn't embarrass herself by getting sick. When she spied Jillian coming her way, Elle plastered on a smile.

Jillian murmured a quick greeting to Brennan before directing her attention to her sister. "Honey, are you okay?"

"I'm fine." She lapsed into introductions. "Brennan, this is my sister, Jillian Sanders."

"It's nice to meet you, Brennan."

Elle noticed that Jillian's smile didn't quite reach her eyes. Like everyone else in her family, she didn't care much for Brennan at this moment. They would all sit back for now—giving him a chance to prove himself.

"You, too." Again, Brennan's automatic response.

"Are you sure you're okay?" Jillian asked. "I can take you home if you'd like."

Wearing a blank expression, Brennan watched Elle as if awaiting her response.

She shook her head no. "I'm feeling much better now."

"Okay. Just let me know if you change your mind."

"I will," Elle promised.

When they were alone once more, Brennan stated, "I don't think your sister likes me."

"Why would you think that? It just takes a while for Jillian to warm up to people. Once she gets to know you—"

He cut her off by saying, "It doesn't matter. I'm not here to make friends."

Her smoldering gaze flicked up to meet his. "Please remember that you're talking about my family."

"What? I haven't said anything negative about them. I'm just not one of those people who allows family to dictate how I live my life. I hope you aren't, either."

Her arms folded across her chest, and her small chin tilted out at him. "My family's not like that," Elle blurted out.

"I'm glad to hear that." In a surprise move, Brennan leaned over to whisper, "What are you doing after the wedding?"

"Nothing. I just plan on going home and getting into bed. This has been a long day for me, and I'm really tired."

The deep timbre of his bass voice became husky. "Think I can change your mind? We haven't seen each other in months."

Elle was speechless for a moment. How could Brennan think that she would fall into bed with him after the way he'd walked out on her? She felt fury, hurt, and a host of other emotions all at once.

"Did you hear me?"

She concentrated on not letting her reaction show. "I heard you." Elle kept her face blank. "I'm sorry, Brennan, but I don't think it would be a good idea."

Sitting up straight in his chair, Brennan frowned, and his eyes narrowed fractionally. "Are you upset with me?"

"No. Why would I be?" Elle's throat tightened. "Could it be because you left the country without a word to me? Not even a good-bye. Or is it because you never called, faxed, e-mailed, or even thought enough of me to send a postcard?"

A muscle leaped in Brennan's jaw, but his voice was soft and even. "You're right, Elle. I didn't handle this well, and my behavior is inexcusable."

"Well, at least you have the guts to admit it." Elle stood up, moving with slow, deliberate motions. Any sudden moves these days caused dizziness. "It's good seeing you again, Brennan," she said faintly. "Let's just leave it at that."

He stood, too. "Will you at least give me a chance to make it up to you?"

"We'll see." Holding her head up high, Elle crossed the room to join her family. She sat down beside her mother in a chair that had recently been vacated by her brother Laine.

"He's a very handsome man," Amanda Ransom acknowledged.

Elle agreed. "He's hard to take sometimes, but I'm crazy about him, Mama."

"I gather you didn't tell him about the baby."

"No, I didn't. This is not the time or place."

"Are you going to tell him?" her mother asked.

"Right now, I don't know."

"He may be a jerk, but he does have a right to know about the baby."

Elle shifted uncertainly. "I know. I just don't know when or how I'm going to tell him."

A heavy silence fell.

"What do you think he'll do?" Carrie asked.

Elle met her sister-in-law's gaze. "I'm not expecting him to jump up and down or anything like that. I suspect Brennan will be shocked."

"Do you think he'll take on an active role in the baby's life?" Allura questioned. "It would be a shame if he didn't."

"Stop putting those negative thoughts out there," Jillian suggested. "Elle won't know anything until she and Brennan have a chance to talk."

"Would you all just drop it?" Elle snapped irritably. "I can handle my own business." Deep down , she didn't feel so confident. With Brennan suddenly back in Los Angeles, it made her situation a little more difficult.

Elle had no idea how he would handle the news of her pregnancy. It wasn't a topic they'd ever discussed. In fact, they'd used protection. But then there was that one night the condom broke . . . now she was pregnant.

The conversation going on around Elle sounded like a low buzz. She had no interest in whatever her family was talking about. Elle's mind was on Brennan and his unexpected reappearance. Why had he come back now?

A twist of conscience surprised Brennan as he stole a look at Elle. He'd hurt her deeply by his leaving; the evidence was etched in her face.

The silver gown she wore accented her slender body,

although her hips seemed more rounded than he remembered. Elle's soft brown shoulder-length hair was piled in loose curls atop her head, lengthening the sweep of her neck and giving her an appearance of height she did not possess.

Their eyes met and held.

Elle was furious with him. Brennan decided he hadn't handled this situation well. Not knowing what else to do, he smiled.

She responded with a tentative smile before turning her attention back to her family.

Brennan recognized the desire that coursed through his body. Elle possessed big, beautiful bedroom eyes and a pair of full, kissable lips that could break the heart of a man . . . if that man actually allowed her passage through the brick wall he called a heart.

Having grown up in a loveless home, Brennan feared he wasn't capable of loving and being loved. It was an emotion totally foreign to him, yet he could not forget the way she made him feel.

The entire time he'd been in Europe, Brennan had had no luck escaping his memories of Elle. She'd stayed on his mind constantly. There were many times he'd wanted to pick up the phone and beg her to join him. There were days he'd just needed to hear her voice. . . .

He didn't like the road his thoughts were traveling. Mentally, he retreated. Brennan fought the urge to walk across the room and ask Elle to leave the reception with him a second time, and common sense won out.

He stayed until after Nyle and Chandra's first dance as husband and wife. Brennan soon decided he'd had enough of the fanfare and stood. He headed to the nearest exit door. Just before he left, Brennan tossed a

.look over his shoulder and found Elle watching him. A faint smile curved his mouth and he waved to her.

She waved back.

Brennan spent the rest of his evening at his Malibu home, listening to music. On nights like this, he turned up the volume on his CD player and relived a time when he'd been truly happy. A time when he'd felt content and his soul had been at peace.

Chapter Two

Turning off her laptop computer, Elle stretched and yawned. She'd gotten up early to attend the eight o'clock service at church and afterward, she'd spent the rest of the morning working on a promotional tour for one of the label's newest acts.

She was exhausted. Elle hadn't slept well last night. Ever since she ran into Brennan yesterday at Nyle's wedding, her thoughts had been troubled and her emotions in turmoil.

Placing her hands on her belly, she whispered, "Your daddy's back, sweetheart. I'm just not sure what it all means. I wish I could tell you that he's going to be a part of our lives. The truth is that I really don't know. I don't know if he's come back to love me or to destroy me."

Elle's behavior at the reception stayed with Brennan throughout the entire weekend. He had expected her to be thrilled at seeing him again. Instead, she'd left him completely baffled. Even disappointed. He'd expected her to be mad at first but . . .

Brennan refused to speculate why he was bothered at all by Elle's apparent lack of interest. He wasn't supposed to care what she thought of him. But he did. He also didn't like the fact that she was angry with him, although she had every right to be. It bothered him that she had built a wall around herself and would not allow him entrance. This was not the same woman he'd left behind. She had changed.

His troubled thoughts of Elle carried over to Monday morning. Brennan had just gotten off the phone with Malcolm after scheduling a time for lunch. He looked forward to seeing his friend, but he was hoping for a chance meeting with Elle, too.

By the time Brennan arrived at Jupiter Records, he fully expected to run into Elle, but was disappointed. Today, she'd decided to work from home.

While Malcolm was on the telephone, he settled onto the plush leather sofa in the large corner office with a picturesque view of Beverly Hills. Brennan stared up at the numerous eight-by-ten black-and-white glossies of various recording artists. His eyes landed on one in particular. The one with him and Malcolm, surrounded by members of their band. Next to it was the one gold record they'd earned.

It all seemed like a lifetime ago.

When Malcolm hung up, Brennan asked, "What's up with your publicist? Elle shot me down at her brother's wedding."

Looking away from his monitor, Malcolm gave Brennan a sidelong glance. "What did you expect?"

Brennan nodded. "She made it clear that she was angry with me."

Pushing his glasses back up, Malcolm grinned. "Surely you're not surprised? Man, you just upped and left the country without a word to her. You left me to do the dirty work. I told her that you had an emergency situation involving the fragrance division in France. I guess when she never heard from you, Elle kind of figured out the truth."

"I thought maybe enough time had passed and she would be a little more forgiving. I even thought she might be happy to see me."

Malcolm's smile disappeared. "Elle was really hurt, Brennan." He leaned forward in his chair. "How long do you plan to stay around this time? If you're not going to be here—leave her alone. Don't play games with Elle. She doesn't deserve that."

He met his friend's gaze. "You know I'm not about games. Malcolm, you know why I had to leave. If I'd stayed it would have only hurt her more. And you're right. Elle doesn't deserve that."

"Yeah, I know why you left, but I still don't think it was right. I'm not even sure Elle would give you a second chance now anyway."

"Why do you say that? Is she seeing someone?"

"I think so. At first I thought the baby was yours, but when she didn't say anything to me, I figured I was wrong about—"

"*Baby?*" Brennan interrupted. "*What baby?*"

"Elle's pregnant," Malcolm announced. "I heard her talking on the phone one evening with her sister."

As their eyes met, Brennan felt a shock run through him. "How far along is she?"

"I don't know. Why?"

Brennan counted back on numbed fingers. "She'd have to be about three or four months right now if the baby was mine."

Malcolm shrugged. "I don't know. She's been very quiet about this."

"You mean she hasn't said anything to you?" Brennan questioned.

Shaking his head, Malcolm replied, "Not a word. Like I told you, Elle's been real quiet. Eventually, she'll tell me something."

"Well, I'm not waiting." Brennan grabbed his car keys off Malcolm's desk. "We're going to have to reschedule lunch."

"Where are you going?"

"I'm going to find out what's going on with Elle Ransom."

He left Jupiter Records, driving in the direction of Elle's house. The conversation he'd had with Malcolm played over and over again in his mind.

Was Elle pregnant with his child? If so, what was he going to do about it? What was he willing to do about the situation?

By the time Brennan pulled into Elle's driveway, he was trying to imagine what his future was going to be like. He climbed out of the car and headed to the front door, his shoulders slumped like a man going to his doom.

Brennan punched the doorbell impatiently. After a series of clicks, the door opened.

He scanned Elle from head to toe, not missing the relaxed look of her tunic-length pullover top and her cropped pants. Raising his eyes back to her face, he asked, "Are you pregnant?"

* * *

"Hello to you, too." Elle stepped back to allow Brennan entrance into her house. *How in the world did he find out?* she wondered nervously.

Brennan met her startled eyes with a steady gaze. *"Are you?"* he demanded.

Elle hesitated, then said, "Yes."

He leaned against the wall, dazed. With visible effort, Brennan pulled his gaze back to hers. "How far along?"

Folding her arms across her chest, Elle asked, "Aren't you being just a little bit too personal?"

"I do not have time for games, Elle. Now, I would like to know if you're carrying my child or whether—"

She reeled slightly. "You can hold it right there, Brennan. First of all, I've only been involved with one man, and that man is you. You are still the only man in this world who knows me so intimately. Now, to answer your question—yes, the baby I'm carrying is yours."

"When were you planning to tell me?"

"I wasn't," Elle confessed. "At least not initially. You'd moved to France, remember?"

Brennan looked fierce, his eyes unreadable and his jaw set. "I had a right to know."

"There was no forwarding address."

"There was always Malcolm," he shot back. "He knew how to contact me."

Elle kept her gaze lowered. If she was trying to look repentant, she failed.

"Look at me," Brennan demanded.

Elle refused to look up.

Raw anger in his voice, he asked, "Why not?"

Swallowing hard, Elle responded. "Do you have any

idea how humiliating this whole ordeal has been for me?''

Brennan's steady gaze made her want to confess everything. "I'd been dumped and I certainly didn't want to go to your best friend. You sent me a message and, believe me, *I got it.*"

"And what was that?"

"That whatever we shared was over," Elle stated without emotion.

Dryly, he said, "I have already apologized for that, Elle. I can't go back and change the past. However, the fact remains that we created a child together. I won't let my child grow up a bastard. My child will not grow up without his father."

She looked up and her throat closed. Elle was thoroughly confused. "What exactly are you saying?"

His eyes narrowed. "I thought it was clear. There's going to be another wedding. *Ours.*"

Elle felt the blood drain from her face. Brennan had caught her completely by surprise. Never in a million years had she expected those words to come out of his mouth. She'd been dreaming about marrying him for over two years, but now . . . She swallowed slowly. "You can't be serious, Brennan."

"*I'm very serious.* We are getting married, and I want to do it before you start showing." Brennan's eyes fell to her stomach.

"I'm three months pregnant," she replied in response to his silent question. "I found out two days after you left."

"That doesn't leave us much time. I hope you can plan a wedding in a matter of weeks. I'll hire a wedding consultant to help you."

Leaning against the back of a chair for support, Elle

uttered, "Brennan, there's only one thing you haven't considered."

"What's that?"

"How do you know I want to marry you?"

Brennan looked as though he hadn't considered the thought. "If you think I'm looking for love, you're wrong, Elle. However, I'm not a man to walk away from my responsibility. Understand that I will not be a part-time father. I do care a great deal for you and I enjoy your company. I believe we will make a good match and that's enough for me. In view of our predicament, I hope that you will feel the same way."

She needed to have her head examined, Elle surmised. She couldn't believe she was even considering his proposal, if you could even call it that. It was to be strictly a marriage of convenience. Could she live with that? She loved Brennan beyond reason, but he did not return that love. And then there was the fact that he mentioned not being a part-time father. It could only mean that he would fight her for custody. Well, Elle wasn't going to be a part-time parent, either. There was only one thing she could do.

"Elle?" Brennan prompted. "Do you have an answer for me?"

She nodded. "I'll marry you," she said quietly.

"We'll have a good life, Elle," he reassured her. "You will have the best of everything. Good doctors—"

She met his gaze with an arched brow. "I like my doctor fine, Brennan. I don't want another one. As a matter of fact, I don't need anything. I have everything under control."

"We'll talk more about this tonight." Brennan headed to the front door, then stopped. Turning around, he asked, "Have you eaten?"

"No," Elle replied. "I was just about to fix a salad before you came."

"Come on. I'm taking you out to lunch, and then we'll start planning our wedding. We have a lot to do. I want to be married within the next month," he announced.

Elle stared wordlessly across at him, her heart pounding. Her dream was about to come true, and it had her feeling vaguely frightened in a nameless way.

For a moment, Brennan studied her intently. "You should eat," he pointed out.

Elle stared down at her meal. The pasta dish had looked so appetizing on the menu but now . . .

"Is something wrong?" he asked her, his eyes narrowing.

"No. It's just . . ." She paused. "Seeing it now in front of me—well, I feel nauseous."

"I'll have the waiter take it away and bring you something else."

"Don't make a fuss, Brennan. I'll just eat it later when I'm feeling better."

Truly concerned for her well-being, he pushed further. "Elle, you need to eat. I've never been pregnant, but I do believe you have to eat properly and take care of yourself."

"I'll try a bowl of soup. Nothing too heavy."

He awarded her a big smile. "That's better."

Brennan couldn't deny he loved taking care of Elle. She was shy and soft-spoken. A gentle spirit. Except when it came to business. When it came to her job, she was like a tigress.

He thought about the baby she carried. Elle had

planned to raise the child without him, and the thought tore at his insides. Brennan truly believed that if he hadn't reappeared in her life, he probably wouldn't have knowledge of his impending fatherhood.

Elle leaned back in her chair, her hand on her stomach as if to apologize. She looked up to find Brennan watching her.

She still looked a little pale, prompting him to ask, "Are you feeling any better?"

She smiled and nodded. She stuck a spoonful of soup into her mouth. She didn't stop eating until the bowl was empty. By the time she was done, Brennan thought she looked much better. "You're not looking as pale as you did earlier."

"I guess I just needed to eat something."

"It's important that you keep up your strength. You should probably eat three meals daily—"

Elle shook her head. "I can't eat like that. I usually eat around four or five times daily. Only in small portions though. It's easier to keep the food down."

"I'm relieved to hear that you're taking care of yourself."

Brennan signaled for the check. A few minutes later, they were back in the car and heading toward the 10 Freeway.

"Where are we going now?"

"Back to your place," Brennan answered. "We might as well go over our wedding. I'd planned to go by my office today, but it can wait. This is far more important." He ignored the fear that stirred within.

When Elle arrived at work the next day, she found Malcolm waiting for her. He followed her into her office.

"You had my man worried."

Putting her briefcase on a nearby chair, she said, "Brennan's fine. You don't have to worry about him."

Malcolm closed the door so they wouldn't be overheard.

Frowning, Elle asked, "Is something wrong?"

"I told Brennan about your pregnancy."

She was floored. "You know?"

Malcolm nodded. "I overheard you on the phone one evening. It was quite by accident, I assure you." He pushed his shoulder-length dreadlocks away from his face and sank down in a nearby chair.

Elle felt guilty. "I'm sorry I didn't come to you. I was going to, but ..." She paused. "Well, it was complicated."

"Because Brennan is the father."

Nodding, Elle stated, "I was so hurt by the way things ended with us. I didn't know how I was going to handle the situation. I'm really sorry, Malcolm. We've worked together too long for me to treat you this way."

He laughed. "It's okay. I understand." Malcolm stood up. "I take it you and Brennan have had some dialogue."

"We have. In fact, you might want to sit back down."

He looked puzzled. "What's going on?"

Elle was doing her best to appear at ease. "Brennan and I talked about the baby and about us. He asked me to marry him."

Malcolm dropped back down into the chair. His eyes were wide in his astonishment, causing Elle to burst into laughter.

"We're getting married."

"Congratulations. I'm happy for you bo—" Malcolm stopped short. "Elle, this is what you want, isn't it?"

She nodded. "You know how much I love Brennan."

"Yeah, I do," was Malcolm's quiet response.

"He seems excited about the baby," she offered.

"Brennan's always wanted children."

But he's never wanted a wife, Elle silently finished for him.

"He needs a woman like you. Congratulations again."

"Thank you, Malcolm."

Their conversation turned to business. A few minutes later, Elle was left alone in her office. She passed the first half hour of her morning jotting notes in her Day-Timer.

The rest of the day was spent performing various duties. She figured if she stayed busy, there would be no time to think of Brennan.

The week breezed by because Elle was immersed in several different projects. By the weekend, she was bone-tired and still feeling ambivalent over her decision to marry Brennan.

Elle needed someone to talk to, so she drove the half-hour distance to Kaitlin's house, nestled in Baldwin Hills. Matt was pulling out of the driveway when she arrived.

"Hey, you taking care of yourself?" he called out to her.

Grinning, she shouted, "I am. Where are you heading?"

"Your brothers and I are going to play some ball for a little bit."

"Have fun. Tell everyone I said hello."

"I will." Matt drove off.

Kaitlin answered the door on the first ring. She had

just given Travaile her bath. "Look who's here, sweetie. Your Auntie Elle is here."

They played with the baby until she became sleepy and irritable. Singing softly, Elle rocked Travaile to sleep, while her sister readied the crib.

"Have you spoken to Brennan since the wedding?" Kaitlin asked after she put her daughter down for a nap.

Elle nodded. "Several times actually. He's called me almost every day."

Kaitlin was clearly surprised. "Really? So, what does he want? Probably trying to get you back into his bed."

"He knows about the baby."

"*How?*" Heading into the kitchen, Kaitlin added, "Come in here with me. I want to hear all about this reunion."

"I don't know how he found out. I didn't really get around to asking him." Elle followed her sister.

"Why not?"

"Brennan wants to get married. He wants to have a quick wedding before I start showing."

"Oh?" Kaitlin pulled out two cans of tuna from the pantry. "So, did you turn him down?"

Elle shook her head no. "I agreed to it, Kaitlin. Brennan and I are getting married. I've dreamed of this for such a long time and now it's finally happening."

Kaitlin surveyed her face. "You don't sound too happy about this. Elle, you don't have to marry Brennan if you don't want to."

"You don't understand. I want to marry him, Kaitlin. I really do—I just wish it weren't going to be a marriage of convenience."

"A marriage of . . ." Kaitlin was shaking her head. "Don't do this, sis. I really don't want to see you get hurt. Please don't do this."

Elle washed her hands in the sink. After drying them with a paper towel, she responded, "My baby deserves a father." She turned sharply in defiance and strode over to the fridge.

"Can you grab the mayo and relish?" Kaitlin asked from across the gourmet kitchen. Along with the items Kaitlin asked for, Elle also grabbed a tomato and a head of lettuce.

Strolling over to where Kaitlin was standing, Elle handed the items to her sister, who said, "Brennan can still be a father. He just won't be in the same home with you and the baby."

Elle grabbed a knife and began slicing the tomato. "I'm afraid he might try to take the baby away from me. Brennan is a very rich and powerful man." She caught her breath in an anxious moment. "I won't take the chance of him gaining custody of my child." Elle averted her eyes to shield her anxieties.

"You're really afraid of him."

"A little," Elle admitted. Her hands trembled slightly and she refused to meet Kaitlin's gaze. "But don't forget how much I love him. I *want* to be with Brennan."

"There is no way we would let him take your child. Look, sis, I know you love him, but he may not deserve you or your love. Talk to John and Laine about this before you do something foolish."

"I know Brennan won't hurt me. He's a little territorial at times, but I can handle that. Who knows? He and I may be fine. He might actually fall in love with me— it has been known to happen."

"Are you willing to risk it?"

"Yes. For my baby's sake, I'll risk anything—even heartache."

Chapter Three

Nothing could have prepared Brennan for the sudden turn of events. He was going to be a father. Just the thought was overwhelming enough. Although he feared he would not be a good father, Brennan was determined not to follow in his parents' footsteps. He would do his best to become a good role model for his child.

He parked beside the silver Jaguar that belonged to his father. Brennan climbed out of his Range Rover and ran up the three steps leading to the porch of his parents' home.

The twelve-thousand-square-foot Mediterranean-style residence with stained-glass windows was located in private and secure Fremont Place in Los Angeles. He was greeted by the housekeeper, who led him through the house and onto the veranda.

"Morning, everyone," Brennan called out as he strode toward the table where his family had gathered for breakfast.

"What's brought you out here so early?"

He smiled. "I came to see you, Aunt Pookie." Pookie Lake was his mother's youngest sister. She and Brennan had always been very close, more like best friends.

Pushing away a stray ebony curl, Pookie laughed. "Boy, I know you better than that. You didn't come here at the crack of dawn just to see me."

Laughing, Brennan breezed through French doors to wash his hands in the kitchen. He returned a few minutes later and sat down in one of the wrought-iron chairs next to his father. "Are you coming into the office today?" he asked.

Brennan Edward Cunningham II laid down the newspaper he'd been reading. "No, not today."

His father didn't like to speak more than was necessary, so Brennan adjusted his own personality to deal more effectively with his father. He reached for a muffin while a maid poured him a glass of apple juice.

Dabbing at the corner of her mouth with a linen napkin, Elizabeth stated, "Son, I have to admit that I'm just as curious as Pookie. Why are you here so early? This isn't like you."

Tapping the multicolored glass pieces that created the mosaic tabletop, Brennan doubted his mother really knew anything about him.

Elizabeth Lake Cunningham was one of those self-absorbed women. A woman with a strong false sense of self. He didn't hate his mother. He loved her very much—he'd just learned to do so from a distance. Brennan felt the same way about his father. Growing up, Pookie had been the one who'd showered him with love and affection, but Brennan still craved the unconditional love of his parents. Now, at the age of thirty-eight, he decided he could do just as well without love.

"Come on, handsome, tell Pookie what's going on in that head of yours."

"I'm getting married," Brennan announced without preamble.

While Pookie clapped her hands with glee, Elizabeth blanched. "This is a horrid little joke, Brennan."

He met his mother's hard gaze with his own. "I can assure you it's no joke, Mother."

Letting the newspaper drop down on the table, his father sat there staring at Brennan, his face frozen in shock.

"So, who is the lucky young lady?" Pookie asked. "And don't tell me you're marrying that Charis Wentworth." Frowning, she added, "I can't stand that sneaky heifer."

Brennan bit back his laughter. "It's not Charis. The woman I'm marrying is Elle Ransom. Her twin brother married Chandra."

"Oh, that's right. She was one of the bridesmaids. The shy one. I saw you two talking during the reception. I'd assumed you'd just met her." Pookie handed her glass to the maid standing nearby. "I would like more cranberry juice, dear."

Brennan shook his head. "I've known Elle for almost four years. We started dating late last year. There's something else you all should know."

"You mean there's more?" Elizabeth quipped.

"Yes." He couldn't hide his grin. "I'm also going to become a father."

Reaching over and squeezing his hand, Pookie murmured, "Congratulations, honey. I'm so happy for you."

Elizabeth was clearly not pleased. "How do you know the baby is yours?" she blurted out. "Surely the girl is not stupid. She knows—"

"Elle's nothing like that," Brennan shot back.

"How can you be so sure?" Elizabeth was not going to let up. "It's not like you've just recently acquired a fortune. You've always been rich."

"Being rich don't make him a fool."

Glaring at her sister, Elizabeth snapped, "Pookie, why don't you stay out of this?"

Brennan ground his teeth in frustration. "Why don't *you* stop trying to play mama all of a sudden? It's a little too late for that, Mother, don't you think?"

Pookie burst into high-pitched laughter.

Slapping her napkin down on the table, Elizabeth rose to her feet. "I'll not be talked to any old way in my own home." She stormed through the open French doors leading into the house.

Mimicking her, Pookie burst into another round of laughter. "Lizbeth needs to lighten up some. She's much too stiff."

"She needs to mind her own business," Brennan snarled. How could she presume to tell him who he should or should not marry?

"She's your mother, Brennan."

He glanced over at the man who'd spoken. "I'm well aware of that, Father. And I still feel the same way. She should mind her own business." He refused to be intimidated by his father. Those days were over.

Picking up his coffee cup, the elder Cunningham took a long sip. Looking into his son's eyes, he said, "In this day and age, you don't have to marry the woman you impregnate."

"I intend to marry Elle," Brennan stated firmly. "Nothing or no one is going to stop me."

"I'm not trying to stop you, son. Just letting you know what your options are."

"Perhaps Brennan loves the girl," Pookie suggested.

His eyes met hers and held. How could he tell her that love had nothing to do with it?

Elle had agreed to meet with Brennan after work. They were going to have a quiet dinner at his house and then go over more wedding plans.

On the northern edge of Los Angeles, Malibu hugged the California shoreline. Elle loved the city because privacy was fiercely guarded in a setting of natural beauty.

She sat in her car admiring the view of Brennan's incredible oceanfront estate, located within the exclusive community of Paradise View. Elle had visited several times in the past, but this time things were different. This would soon become her home.

Elle exhaled slowly before climbing out of the car. A few minutes later, she found herself knocking on the front door. As an afterthought, she rang the doorbell.

Brennan's housekeeper opened the door. Seeing Elle, she grinned. "Miss Ransom, it's so good to see you again."

Embracing the portly woman, she murmured, "It's wonderful to see you, too, Melina."

Elle stepped into the familiar grandeur of Brennan's seven-thousand-four-hundred-square-foot home. The living room featured a twenty-foot cathedral ceiling, an ocean-view balcony, glass archways, and Italian marble floors. She walked past the formal dining room, where there was a table that could easily seat forty guests comfortably.

Elle peeked into the kitchen. "Is Robert still working here?" She gave the housekeeper a knowing smile.

"Yes, he's still here." Melina laughed. "He and I got married right before Mr. Cunningham returned."

Elle hugged Melina. "Congratulations."

She was taken to the media room, where Brennan was watching television. He looked up from his seat when she walked in. Quickly rising to his feet, Brennan kissed her.

"I was getting worried about you." He led her over to the love seat.

Elle sat down, saying, "I've been here awhile, but I didn't get out of the car right away."

"Why?" Brennan eased down beside her.

"The view is exquisite. I just wanted to enjoy it for a while."

She was nervous.

Brennan must have sensed it, because he took her hand in his and began stroking it.

Elle glanced up at him and smiled, then looked away.

"Why are you so nervous?" he asked gently. "Do I scare you now?" Brennan's lips seared her ears.

She tried to turn her head away, but it was no use— he held her fast, and his mouth covered her parted lips in a scorching kiss that made her tremble. She determinedly clamped her lips together.

Brennan was just as willful as she. She could feel his tongue trying to gain entrance. Desire shuddered through her. Elle was suddenly aware of her vulnerability.

His kisses made her senses spin, left her weak and trembling in his arms, so that Brennan had to hold her up.

Meeting her gaze, he whispered huskily, "Why don't you stay for the night?"

"It's tempting," Elle admitted. "But I think I'll pass."

Brennan sat up straight. "May I ask why? After all, we are going to be married—not to mention we are expecting a child."

Placing a hand on her chest, Elle replied, "I . . . this is going so fast for me, I can barely catch my breath. I need some time."

"I'm sorry I hurt you, Elle. I didn't want to . . ."

She stood up. "It has nothing to do with that. I just need some time to adjust." Elle glanced around the room. "To all this. It's all so overwhelming."

Melina eased into the room. "Dinner is ready, Mr. Cunningham."

He nodded and stood up. "I had Robert make beef Stroganoff."

It was one of Elle's favorites. She smiled, touched that he remembered.

Over dinner, Brennan and Elle discussed plans for their wedding. Both had agreed on a short and informal ceremony in the rose garden on his estate. Afterward, they settled into the media room.

"I spoke with my attorney yesterday and, upon his advice, I had him prepare a prenuptial agreement. I want you to take a look at it and tell me what you think."

"I can tell you now what I think. I think prenuptial agreements imply that the marriage is doomed to fail."

He opened his mouth to speak, but Elle held up her hand to stop him. "I'm going to sign it. However, I want you to know that I don't want anything from you. Not in the material sense, anyway."

"Once you read it, you'll see that I've been very generous—"

"I mean it, Brennan. If our marriage doesn't work out, I don't want your money."

"You have the child to think about."

"Are you planning to divorce me?"

Her question caught him off guard. "No."

"Then it really doesn't matter what those papers say. Do you have a pen?"

"Elle, you really should read them first," he advised. "You never sign anything without reading it."

"I intend to make this marriage work, Brennan." She quickly signed the legal document. "I'm counting on you to do the same." Elle held the papers out to him.

Brennan took them, then promptly dropped them on the desk. He pulled Elle into his arms. "I hope you're not always this hardheaded. Aren't you just a tiny bit curious about the settlement? You could be left with nothing."

She stepped out of Brennan's embrace. "Then it's the same thing I started with. Can't miss something I never had."

"When you move in here, your life is going to change."

"Not if I can help it. Brennan, my life's not bad now. I may not have your wealth, but I live very comfortably."

"I understand that and I don't mean to imply otherwise. I'm just saying that—"

"I know what you're trying to say," Elle interrupted. "I'm happy with my lifestyle the way it is. I intend to stay grounded in who I am and where I come from."

"Enough of this conversation." Leaning forward, he kissed her. "Have you told your family yet?"

"No. I'm going to do it when I see them this weekend. It's easier when we're all together. One of my sisters already knows, but she's been sworn to secrecy." Inclining her head, Elle asked, "What about you?"

"My family knows."

"But they're not happy about it, are they?"

"Pookie's very excited. Dad is Dad and my mother—well, she'll get used to the news."

Elle laid her head on his shoulder. "You never did tell me how you liked living in France."

For the rest of the evening, Brennan talked about his time abroad. Elle itched to ask why he'd decided to leave so abruptly, but wisely held her tongue. She had a feeling that he would eventually open up to her. It had been this way between them in the past. As they'd gotten to know each other better, Brennan had begun to open up more and more. Then, out of the blue, he'd disappeared.

Six days later, Elle told the rest of her family about the engagement. It was Daisi's birthday, and her brother Garrick had conspired with their mother to throw a surprise party for his wife.

"Have you lost your ever-loving mind?" Ivy screamed.

Amanda held up a hand. "Ivy, stop yelling, for goodness sake. We can all hear you and so can the neighbors. Elle's business doesn't need to be all over the neighborhood."

Giving her mother a grateful smile, Elle whispered, "Thanks, Mama."

Ivy wasn't going to let the subject drop. "Excuse me, but is everyone okay with Elle marrying a man who doesn't love her?"

"The only person who has to be okay with this is Elle," Jillian answered. "This is a decision only she can make."

"I agree with Ivy. Elle should just have her baby and not worry about that . . ." Ray's voice died when he caught his mother's warning glare.

"I've already told you all that this is my business."
Elle sighed loudly. "I wish I hadn't opened the floor
for discussion. For the last time, I am not going to
jeopardize the custody of my baby. If I don't marry
Brennan, I'm afraid he'll try to take the baby from me.
He doesn't want to be a part-time parent, and neither
do I."

"We could fight him—" Laine began.

"But could you guarantee me a win?" Elle cut in.
When he remained silent, she continued, "Brennan
comes from a very rich and powerful family."

Carrie glanced over at Chandra. "How well do you
know the Cunninghams?"

"I've known them all of my life, and Elle's right.
Brennan *will* want to raise his child."

The room grew silent.

"If Brennan wants to marry you, Elle, then he must
care for you," Regis offered. She ran a hand over her
own rounded belly. "Everything could turn out for the
best."

Elle met her sister-in-law's gaze. "I almost wish your
sister was in town. I sure could use Sabrina's psychic
vibes right now." A smile tugged at her mouth as she
watched Laine place a loving hand over Regis's.

Sabrina had been right in her prediction. In July,
Laine and Regis would have another child.

Ivy cut into her thoughts. "Well, I think you're crazy
for even considering this. I would think you'd want
more."

"And I think you'd be a lot better off if you'd worry
about your own marriage. From the looks of it, that
should be your main focus," Elle retorted. She instantly
regretted her comment when she saw how hurt Ivy
looked. "I'm sorry. I shouldn't have said that."

"No, it's okay. I'm sure everyone has noticed Charles's absences." Ivy's eyes suddenly filled with tears. "You all might as well know. Charles is moving out today. He'll be gone by the time the children and I get home tonight."

The room was soaked in silence once more. Amanda walked over to Ivy and embraced her. Suddenly Ivy burst into heartrending sobs.

Elle felt her own eyes water. She'd suspected that Charles and Ivy were having problems, but never had she imagined him leaving. He and Ivy had been together since their sophomore year in high school.

Amanda took Ivy to her bedroom.

"I feel awful," Elle murmured.

"Ivy knows you didn't mean anything by it," Jillian reassured her. "She's going through a bad patch, but it'll all work out. She and Charles probably need some time apart."

The minutes ticked by slowly as they all waited for Amanda and Ivy to return. Elle only half listened to the conversation going on between Jillian, Regis, and Carrie. Allura had gone into the kitchen to check on dinner and the men were outside on the patio.

Chandra touched her hand. "Brennan is a sensible man. He'll understand if you decide not to rush into a marriage."

Elle nodded.

When she could wait no longer, Elle stood up and headed to her mother's room. She needed to clear the air with her sister.

She knocked softly before she stuck her head inside. "Can I come in?"

"Come on in, baby. I was just about to check on dinner." Amanda rose slowly, using her quad cane for support. "You two can chat until it's time to eat."

She left the room, closing the door quietly behind her.

Elle stood in the middle of the room, staring down at the carpet. She felt bad about her angry words to her sister. How could she have been so cruel? Wrapping her arms around her middle, she asked, "Are you feeling better, Ivy?"

"As well as one can be when her marriage is breaking up, I suppose."

She sat down on the edge of the bed. "I'm so sorry."

Reaching over, Ivy took Elle's hand in her own. "I guess we all can't be lucky in love."

Pulling her hand away, Elle said, "I don't agree. Some of us may have to work a little harder, that's all." It unnerved her to be included in that statement.

"It takes two people to make a marriage work, sis."

"Ivy, I want to ask you something. Do you still love Charles?"

Her sister took a moment to respond. "Yes. He just doesn't love me back."

"I don't believe that."

Ivy wiped at a lone tear slipping down her cheek. "Charles feels we are going in two different directions."

"I hope you two can find your way back to each other."

Swiping at her tears, Ivy replied, "I'm not so sure we can."

Elle embraced her. "Charles still loves you, Ivy. I really believe that."

"You don't know how much I want to hold on to that dream. I love him so much that I can't see my life without him."

Amanda rapped on the bedroom door. "Dinner's ready. Why don't you two come on out?"

Rising to her feet, Elle held out a hand to Ivy. "Come on, sis. Let's get something to eat."

Throughout dinner and most of the evening, Ivy was quiet, much to Elle's dismay. With her own marriage troubled, her sister really believed that Elle's marriage to Brennan was doomed as well. She conceded that it wasn't the most conventional way of doing things, but she had her baby to think about.

Doubt and insecurity plagued Elle throughout her hour-and-a-half drive back to Los Angeles. Maybe marrying Brennan wasn't the smart thing to do right now. Perhaps she needed to give this more thought.

By the time she arrived home, Elle was thoroughly confused. She didn't know what to do about her situation.

Elle hadn't been home thirty minutes when the phone rang. It was Brennan. She tried to sound cheerful.

"What's wrong, Elle? You sound strange."

"I've been doing some thinking. I'm not so sure we're doing the right thing by rushing into marriage."

"Are you trying to back out of the wedding?"

His tone had suddenly become guarded.

"All I'm saying is that maybe we should give it some more thought. I don't want to get married only to have our marriage end in divorce."

"There are no guarantees in life, Elle. What happened today to bring this on?"

"One of my sisters is having marital problems. It really made me rethink our situation."

"Elle, I won't hurt you, if that's what you're thinking. I will make you happy. I will be a good husband and father. I give you my word."

I would rather have your love, she added silently. *How could he doom himself to a life without love?*

Brennan smiled at his assistant. "The ad campaign for Cache Parfum looks great. You did a great job, Kassie."

"Thank you, Brennan." She frowned. "You look tired. Are you feeling okay?"

He nodded. "I've been working late hours on the projections for the new Advantage Cologne." Brennan ran his hand over his face. "My father wants to launch this new line next season."

"Anything I can help you with?"

"I'll let you know. For now I want you to focus all of your attention on Cache."

When Kassie left, Brennan turned to face the picture window in his office. He hated his job as senior vice president of marketing for Cunningham Lake Cosmetics and Fragrances. He'd never wanted to work for his family's company, but agreed to do so because he'd thought it would bring his family closer together.

Brennan decided to play hooky from work for the rest of the afternoon. He drove along the Pacific Coast Highway on his way to his house. The March sun was bright and the weather felt just right.

On impulse, he drove to a nearby park and stopped. Smiling, he watched a father playing with his son. He could see the little boy's adoration for his daddy. As he continued to observe them, Brennan felt the onslaught of heartache. He and his father had never shared such tender moments. His dad had always been too busy with the company.

Too busy to attend any of his school functions, his sports activities—he'd even missed both Brennan's high school and college graduations. His mother had been there, but she'd always seemed bored. Only Pookie, Muffin, and his Uncle Steven had ever appeared to be excited over his achievements.

He vowed that things would be different when his child was born. Brennan resolved to be a husband and a father first. Business would always take second place.

Chapter Four

"Dahling, you can't really mean to wear a St. Charles bridal gown." Bettina made a face. "They are pretty, but you're marrying a Cunningham. Couture is the way to go. . . ."

Kaitlin began to remove her earrings. "I'll show you the way to go—"

Jillian and Ivy had to hold her back while Elle pulled Bettina off to the side. Maybe it hadn't been such a good idea to bring this irritating woman with her to Riverside. "I don't know of any other way to make this any clearer. This *is* my wedding and I'll wear what I want." Gesturing toward Kaitlin, she continued to speak. "My sister is the owner of the St. Charles Bridal Salons, and I happen to love her gowns."

"But you are marrying a Cunningham," Bettina insisted. "Mr. Cunningham has given you a generous allowance. You can spend up to twenty thousand for your wedding gown alone."

"And what exactly is your percentage out of all this?"

Kaitlin demanded. "Is it the standard twenty percent of total wedding costs?"

"Twenty thousand dollars for a dress?" Ivy shook her head in disgust. "You could have your entire wedding cost less than that and it would still be nice."

Jillian nodded in agreement. "Nyle married the mayor's daughter and their wedding came to about forty thousand dollars. I thought they were both crazy to spend so much, but it's what they wanted. Since they are both doctors, I guess they can easily afford it."

"I don't see spending that kind of money for a wedding," Elle agreed. "The dress I want to wear costs fifteen hundred dollars, and that includes the generous discount Kaitlin's given me."

"But . . ." Bettina groaned. "What about Mr. Cunningham?"

"I can buy my own dress, Bettina. If Brennan doesn't want to marry me because my dress isn't a twenty-thousand-dollar one, then so be it." Elle couldn't keep the frustration from her voice. The wedding coordinator Brennan had hired was getting on her nerves. Bettina fought her on everything. Elle wanted a garden wedding, but the bridal consultant decided it should be held at the Beverly Hills Hotel. Their wedding was less than three weeks away and not much had been accomplished.

"May I come in?"

Elle turned around at the sound of Brennan's voice. Walking toward him, she said, "You're just in time. I was just about to fire Bettina."

"*Excuse me?* You're going to fire me? I don't think so. I quit! I won't be a party to a tacky little wedding—"

"Tacky! I'll show you tacky. . . ." Allura jumped to her feet and rushed after the woman, who had suddenly broken into a sprint, leaving behind her expensive shoes. Picking them up, Allura tossed them after Bettina.

Hearing a scream, everyone rushed to the front of the house, leaving Brennan and Elle alone in the den.

Wearing an amused expression, he said, "I gather things didn't go well with Bettina."

Elle was ecstatic to see Brennan. Using her right hand to massage away the beginnings of a tension headache, she replied, "No, they didn't. I've made a decision, though. Kaitlin is going to help me plan our wedding, and I'm wearing one of her gowns. Can we still have the ceremony in your rose garden?"

Brennan nodded. "I want you to be happy. We can get married wherever you like." He reached inside his pocket and pulled out a small velvet box. "No bride should be without an engagement ring." Brennan removed the ring from the case and placed it on Elle's left hand.

"Oh, my Lord." Elle couldn't believe the size of the pear-shaped diamond in the platinum setting. "How many carats is this?"

"Fourteen. Do you like it?"

"Brennan, this is nice. It's really nice, but I couldn't even hold my hand up if I wear this ring. Would you mind very much if I asked for something smaller? *Much smaller.* Like a plain wedding band."

He broke into laughter. "You're not serious, are you?"

"Yes, I am. This is too much for me." She stared down at the beautiful stone embraced by baguettes on each side. "I have small hands. It's too much."

"I think it looks beautiful on your hand, Elle."

Before she could respond, Allura and the others

returned. Brennan held out her hand. "Ladies, what do you think?"

Allura gasped. "Whoa, baby! Boy, that's some ring."

"I was just telling Brennan that I think I should get something smaller," Elle announced.

"Why?" Allura demanded. "I like that one just fine."

Elle glared at her sister. "Jillian, what do you think?" Out of all of her sisters, Jillian had always been the most logical one.

"It's a nice ring. I'm like you, though. I would prefer something a little smaller, too."

Turning to her sister-in-law, Elle asked, "What about you, Regis?"

"The ring is exquisite, but I really think this is something you and Brennan should discuss. *Alone.*"

"You may not want my opinion. However, I'm going to give it anyway," Allura announced. "You really should be more appreciative. The man thought enough of you to even buy a ring."

Kaitlin wrapped an arm around Elle. "I think you and Brennan will find the perfect engagement and wedding rings. I agree with Regis on this. You don't need any advice from us." In a lower voice, she added, "The ring is stunning. Make sure you don't hurt his feelings."

Elle felt so guilty. She hadn't meant to make such a big deal out of the ring. "Brennan, I'm sorry."

"It's okay," he stated. "We'll go tomorrow and pick out another one."

"I really didn't mean to make such a fuss. The ring . . . it's a beauty—"

"I understand." Brennan stroked her cheek. "It's fine."

"Are you sure?"

He smiled then. "Elle, if you want another ring—it's okay. We will get you one tomorrow."

"It's no rush." She placed a hand on her mouth. "I feel so bad about this."

After pulling her hand away, Brennan cupped her face in his palm and raised her head until she looked at him. "You worry too much."

The sunlight streaming into the family room seemed to illuminate his strong features, accenting his sensual chiseled mouth. Elle struggled to ignore the tingling in the pit of her stomach. Her heart jolted and her pulse pounded. Happiness filled her just by being near him. Brennan had unlocked her heart and soul. Everything would be perfect if only he felt the same way about her.

Elle stared up at him with full lips that trembled so much he wanted to still them with his. Brennan kissed her. Once, twice. When her lips parted, he closed his mouth over hers.

He kissed her deeper, pulling her close. Brennan could feel his blood rush and pound through his veins. Her nearness made his senses spin.

The tangible bond that now existed between them gave Brennan the reason he needed to explain away his emotions. He refused to delve any further because then he would find that his feelings for Elle had nothing to do with reason.

Whenever she was around, Brennan struggled to maintain a closed expression, lest Elle get wind of his vulnerability. Her touch could upset his balance.

Staring at the ring box in his hand, Brennan pushed back his confusion. Most women would have dreamed of wearing the ring he'd bought for Elle. Only she had rejected it. She had actually given the ring back to him and asked for a plain wedding band. Was she for real?

As he observed her now with her sisters, Brennan didn't know quite what to make of her. For one thing, he couldn't understand this need of hers to surround herself with family all the time. Elle loved spending time with them while he avoided his own family as much as he could. Brennan enjoyed a warm relationship with Pookie and his uncle's fiancée, Muffin Worthington.

At the sound of footsteps, Brennan looked up to find Elle coming his way. He was suddenly filled with a strange inner excitement.

"Why are you sitting over here by yourself?" she inquired with a smile.

"You were busy with your sisters. I didn't want to get in the way."

Taking him by the hand, Elle pulled him out of the chair. "Brennan, it's your wedding, too. You should be a part of the planning."

He stood rooted to the spot. "You have carte blanche, sweetheart. Do whatever you like." He didn't feel comfortable around the rest of her family.

Her look of disappointment made him quickly amend his statement. "I didn't mean it the way it sounded. What I meant to say was that I'm sure whatever you ladies decide will be fine."

"I'd feel better if you would help me, Brennan," Elle insisted. "It is our wedding. Not just mine."

"I'll give it a shot." Brennan reluctantly followed her into the den, where everyone else was gathered. Jillian offered him a can of soda, but Brennan politely declined.

He sat quietly beside Elle as she scanned through magazine after magazine. He had no idea how he could possibly assist her. In fact, he found this whole process boring.

"What do you think of this dress?" she asked him.

"It's nice." His voice was colored in neutral shades. "Is this the one you want?"

"Yes. Kaitlin was able to order it for me."

"You're going to look stunning. By the way, Mother has offered to host an engagement party in our honor."

"You didn't force her to do any of this, did you?"

"No, actually it was her idea." Frowning, Brennan asked, "Why would you say something like that?"

"I'm just surprised. I got the impression that she didn't care much for me."

"You only saw her at your brother's wedding."

"It was long enough."

Brennan didn't doubt Elle's feelings. His mother made it quite obvious when she didn't care for someone. "It doesn't matter whether Mother likes you or not. You're not marrying her. Now, my aunt, Pookie. She likes you and she thinks we make a good couple. *Attractive couple* were her exact words."

"She's quite a character. Your aunt. I really like her, though." Elle took Brennan's hand in her own. "The two of you are close, aren't you?"

He nodded. "She and Muffin hold special places in my heart."

"Muffin?"

"Yes. She's engaged to my uncle, Steve. You'll meet them at our engagement party." Rising up, he announced, "I need to get back to Los Angeles. I've got a dinner meeting with my dad and my uncle."

Elle walked him to the door. "I'll be home later tonight."

"Should I come over?" The huskiness lingered in his tone. Brennan looked her over seductively.

"If you want to." She gave him a shy smile.

Brennan's hungry gaze raked over her body. "I'll see you around nine." He knew that tonight would be the night they would get reacquainted in the physical sense.

During dinner, he found it hard to stay focused. Brennan's mind was on what would take place later that night when he returned to Elle's. He missed making love to her.

Three hours dragged by before the meeting finally came to an end. Brennan bade his father and uncle good night and drove the short distance back to Elle's house.

He'd barely parked the car when she threw open the door and ran out to him.

"Did you miss me?"

She kissed him. "What do you think?"

Brennan picked Elle up and carried her back inside the house. He put her down briefly to lock the door, then picked her up again. He carried her upstairs and into her bedroom.

He hadn't been inside the room since the night he'd walked out of Elle's life. This time there would be no leaving. Tonight was the beginning of their future together.

The next morning, Brennan drove Elle to Jupiter Records.

"You should have allowed me to take you to breakfast," he stated as he pulled into an empty parking space. "The bagel you just finished isn't going to hold you until lunch."

Elle climbed out of the car. "I'll send out for something if I get hungry."

Brennan followed her into the building. They stopped by Malcolm's office.

"How's the happy couple?" Malcolm asked. "Everything set for the wedding?"

Smiling, Elle answered, "We're getting there."

Picking up a FedEx envelope, he handed it to her. "Your plane ticket arrived late yesterday."

"Thanks." Elle laid it next to her briefcase. She strolled over to the wet bar and poured hot water into a couple of mugs. She dropped one tea bag into each.

"What's the ticket for?" Brennan asked.

Handing him a cup, Elle replied, "I have to go to New York on business." She handed the other cup to her boss.

Brennan eyed his friend. "Elle's pregnant. Why are you sending her to New York?"

Inhaling deeply, Elle answered, "I have a job to do, remember? What's wrong with you, Brennan?"

"I'm not sure you should be traveling as much."

"You're sweet for worrying, but I'm going to be fine," she assured him. "My doctor has already given his approval."

Brennan took a sip of his tea. "I'm going with you then."

"It really isn't necessary, Brennan."

"I'm going. It's settled."

Elle and Malcolm exchanged amused expressions. She was touched by his concern.

Later, in her office, Brennan stated, "I have to be

honest with you. I really don't want you traveling while you're pregnant like this."

"I told you, I've already cleared this with my doctor. I can travel up until my seventh month."

"The doctor may be fine with this, but I'm not."

"Brennan, I appreciate your concern, but please understand and trust that I will be careful. Nothing is going to happen to our baby."

"You can leave this job. Malcolm would understand."

She couldn't believe what she was hearing. "Brennan, I love my job. I'm not interested in leaving. At least not right now."

"Elle—"

She cut him off by holding up her hand. "I'm taking care of myself, Brennan. You have nothing to worry about. I love what I do and I intend to do it as long as I can."

Elle expected to work up until the baby was born. After that, she planned to work from home. One day soon, she and Brennan would have to sit down and continue this discussion, but not today. She had enough on her mind.

I must be out of my mind, Brennan mused as he pulled into the circular driveway of his parents' home. Why had he agreed to have dinner with his mother tonight? His father was away on business, leaving him to deal with her alone. Well, at least he would have Pookie by his side. Brennan smiled. The evening would be entertaining after all.

Instead of using his key, Brennan rang the doorbell. He was greeted immediately by the housekeeper.

"Hello, Brennan. Your mother and aunt are in the library."

"Thank you, Bella." He strode down the long hallway toward the first room on the left. Brennan found his aunt seated on the burgundy leather sofa and Elizabeth standing near the window, her arms folded across her chest.

"Evening, ladies."

Turning around, Elizabeth asked, "How are you, Brennan?"

"I'm fine," he responded. He glanced over to where Pookie was sitting and smiled. She grinned back.

Watching them, Elizabeth cleared her throat noisily. "Dinner should be ready shortly." She moved from the window to the wet bar. "There's something that's been bothering me, Brennan. Do you really have any idea what you're doing? How can you be sure this woman isn't trying to pass off someone else's baby as yours?"

"Do women even do that anymore?" Pookie questioned before taking a sip of wine from her glass. "Especially with the threat of DNA hanging over our heads."

Pouring herself a brandy, Elizabeth sent her sister an irritated look. "Pookie, stay out of this. It really has nothing to do with you." She asked Brennan, "Can I get something for you?"

He shook his head no.

"Lizbeth, you need to get a grip on reality. Brennan is my nephew. I'm interested in his well-being, too."

"You ladies don't have to worry. I've known Elle for a few years now, and she's not like that."

Elizabeth was clearly not convinced. "I'm not so sure." She took a sip of her drink. "A woman will do anything to get what she wants."

"Speaking from experience, Lizbeth, dear?" Pookie inquired.

Elizabeth paled.

"I think Brennan's a smart man, Lizbeth, dear. Surely this little snip of a girl isn't capable of pulling a fast one on our young man here." Standing up, Pookie finished her wine and strolled over to the bar to pour herself another.

"Oh, just be quiet, Pookie. What would you know about anything? Perhaps if you weren't so busy running around here chasing men who are barely out of puberty . . ."

Wearing a wide grin, Pookie stated, "Honey, I'm not ashamed of the fact that I happen to love young men. They are so much easier on the eye." She winked at Brennan playfully. "I've married two men who were much older than me, and look where they are—*dead*. This time around I intend to find a man who stands a good chance of outliving me."

Elizabeth shook her head in disgust. "It's hard to believe that we are related."

"I know," Pookie agreed. "You being such a stick in the mud and all." She gave a mock sigh. "It's a burden I have to bear. . . ."

Brennan burst into laughter. His aunt was giving her sister a fit. They were as different as day and night. Brennan found their constant bickering amusing at times.

"I need to check on dinner." Elizabeth practically ran out of the room.

Still laughing, Pookie placed her empty glass on the marble bar top. "I have to make a quick phone call before we sit down to eat."

She was gone in a flash, leaving him alone.

"Hello, cousin."

Brennan tossed a look over his shoulder. "Jordan, what are you doing here? I'm surprised you're not off somewhere investigating a fire." He and Jordan were as close as brother and sister. He rose to his feet to give her a hug.

"Not tonight. I'm having dinner with you all. After that, Aunt Pookie and I are going to the movies."

"Have fun."

Pushing an errant amber curl out of her eyes, Jordan grinned. "Aunt Elizabeth told me about your engagement. I'm so happy for you." She embraced him. "I would sure love to marry off my brothers."

"You and Aunt Pookie are about the only ones. Mother seems to think I've lost my mind."

"I'm just glad you're not marrying that Charis Wentworth. There's something about her I don't trust." Jordan opened a bottle of Perrier and poured it into a glass.

"Charis and I were not a good match," Brennan confessed. "It would never have worked."

"Do you love Elle? I spoke to a couple of her sisters at Chandra's wedding. We all attended high school together. That was before my mother died and we left Riverside. We kind of lost contact after that. The Ransoms are a real nice family. I used to be crazy about Laine."

"I care for her, Jordan. That's about it. Love is much too overrated."

Shaking her head, she said, "I'm afraid I can't agree with you, Brennan. You really should give love a chance."

"I don't need it. Can't miss what I never had."

Frowning, Jordan stated, "Brennan, honey, I hate it

when you talk this way. You are loved. I, for one, adore you." She gave him one of her bright smiles. "I truly hope you'll find much happiness with Elle Ransom. She seems very genuine, and I'm looking forward to getting to know her."

Later, once they were seated at the dinner table, Brennan said, "Mother, tell me something. Why do you want to host an engagement party if you are so against this wedding?"

"If you insist on seeing this through, then I might as well support you." Elizabeth sighed dramatically.

"I don't want any surprises, Mother."

Picking up her wineglass, Elizabeth took a tiny sip.

Brennan gazed at her for a moment before picking up his knife and fork.

"Aunt Elizabeth, I'd love to help you with the party," Jordan offered.

"Thank you, dear."

Throughout dinner, conversation was stilted. Brennan found his mother constantly watching him. He proceeded to ignore her.

"Brennan, why don't you come to the movies with us? We haven't done anything together like that in a long time."

"I'd love to, but I have a mountain of reports stacked on my desk at home. I have a lot of work to do."

Jordan glanced over at Elizabeth. "I spoke with Daddy, and he's coming home tonight. He said that Uncle Edward's staying for another day or two, and from there he's going to Las Vegas."

Brennan watched his mother's face with interest. She seemed surprised by Jordan's comment. His father frequently made side trips like that. He had often wondered if his father had a mistress. If so, he'd been very successful in keeping her hidden.

Elizabeth sipped her wine. "I expect Edward will call sometime tonight."

After dinner, they settled into the grand family room.

"Dinner was superb," Jordan complimented Elizabeth. "I love prime rib." Pushing away tendrils of wavy hair, she smiled at her cousin. "Brennan, I really wish you would reconsider coming with us. It's been ages."

He shook his head. "I really have a lot of work to do. After the wedding, I want to take some time off."

Elizabeth looked disgusted. "What on earth for? The woman is already pregnant."

Pookie patted Brennan's leg. "Honey, I understand. One can't possibly relate when one lives such a sterile life."

Chapter Five

"My goodness!" Carrie exclaimed as she climbed out of the car. "Will you look at this house! You could put at least five families in here."

Nodding in agreement, Daisi replied, "This is going to be some engagement party."

"Dear heart, the Cunninghams are definitely going all out for Elle and Brennan." Ivy took Bridget out of her car seat. "I don't know that I'll be able to stand all the snobbery."

"All wealthy people aren't snobs," Daisi pointed out. "Some of them are really very nice."

"Then you have the ones that hold their noses so high in the air, if it rained, they'd drown," Ivy countered.

Laughing, Carrie eased her baby out of her seat, prompting a loud protest from the sleeping infant. "Come on, sugar. Mommy's sorry. She didn't mean to wake you. . . ."

Jillian climbed out of her car and walked over to where they were standing. "This is some place, huh?"

"Yes, it is." Daisi pulled on her silk sheath. "We're probably underdressed. Maybe we should have worn something a little more dressy."

Ivy shook her head. "No, the invitation didn't imply that. I think we should be fine. Anyone seen Elle? She's supposed to be meeting us out front."

"Here she comes," Carrie announced.

"Hello, sisters."

"Hey, what about your brothers?" Nyle questioned from behind them. He and Chandra joined the growing circle of Ransoms. "Are we formulating a plan of attack?" he teased.

"Be nice," Elle said with a smile.

"There you are," Brennan stated as he came toward them. "I was starting to think that you'd changed your mind."

She leaned lightly into him, tilting her face toward his. "No, I haven't changed my mind. Just running late."

Brennan wrapped his arms around her midriff.

They all followed him around to the back of the house, where three huge tents had been set up.

Elle glanced around. "Everything is so beautiful."

Brennan's mother had spared no expense, but Elle could not rid herself of the unease she felt. Perhaps it was due to the knowledge that Elizabeth Cunningham didn't care much for her. Elle prayed that one day the woman would come to accept her.

Once Brennan saw that her family members were settled, he pulled Elle off to the side.

"Let's go inside," he whispered in her ear. "I want to spend some time alone with you."

"But I just got here. What in the world will your mother think?"

Brennan's mouth covered hers in response. Parting her lips, Elle raised herself to meet his kiss. Blood pounded in her brain, leaped from her heart, and made her knees tremble.

When they parted, she moved to view herself in the hall mirror. Pulling a tissue out of her purse, Elle wiped off what was left of her lipstick.

Brennan's kiss still singing in her veins, Elle reapplied her lip color. She caught his handsome reflection in the mirror. He was standing there, arms folded across his chest, watching her. Elle turned around.

"Do you think your mother will mind if you gave me a tour of the house?"

"She won't mind. Mother loves to show off this place." Brennan took her by the hand. "Come on."

She was enthralled with the elegant three-storied home. It was obviously beautifully maintained, filled with original priceless art and aristocratic furnishings. The furniture, carpets, and draperies all bespoke refinement and wealth.

Brennan eased an arm around her. "We should join the guests. But before we do—" Leaning down, he kissed her fully on the lips.

Hearing the click of high heels on the marble-tiled floor, Elle pulled away from Brennan.

She took in the sight of the woman coming toward them, dressed in a flowing dress that reached her ankles. It was clear to Elle that the woman only had eyes for Brennan. She recognized Charis Wentworth from the society pages and numerous magazine articles written about her family.

Beside her, Brennan growled, "What is she doing here?"

* * *

Tossing her flowing ebony mane over her shoulders, Charis sashayed toward them. "Brennan, darling, it's wonderful to see you again."

Brennan's mouth tightened. "I thought you were living in Hawaii somewhere."

"Your mother called and told me what was going on, so I came home as soon as I could." Charis smiled and curled her fingers over his forearm, pressing slightly. "Someone needs to talk some sense into you."

Moving slightly out of her reach, Brennan stated, "This is my fiancée, Elle Ransom. Sweetheart, this is Charis Wentworth."

"It's nice to meet you, Charis."

"Yes, I'm sure." Turning her back to Elle, she effectively separated them. She asked Brennan, "Can we please go somewhere and talk?"

Elle was taken aback by her rudeness. Stepping around Charis, she said, "Will you both please excuse me?" Not waiting for a response, she quickly turned on her heel. She couldn't stand being around the woman a moment longer. Charis gave her an uneasy feeling. She was trouble, Elle could sense it.

Brennan stared after Elle for a moment before taking off after her. He caught up with her and asked, "Why are you running away?"

Elle stopped walking and turned around. "It's obvious she needs to talk to you, so I'm giving the two of you some space to do just that. Do whatever it takes to get rid of her. If you don't, then I'm going home. I will not be humiliated, Brennan."

Smiling, he stroked her chin. "There is no need for jealousy."

"I meant what I said. We can call off this charade—"

"Charade. Is this what you think? Elle, I assure you our marriage will be very real. We will be husband and wife in every sense of the word."

"Maybe you should be telling all this to your ex-girlfriend."

"That's exactly what I intend to do." Brennan brushed his lips against hers.

Elle's lips were hesitant against his, as if she were unsure. Then she was kissing him back, robbing him of breath.

Fire burst in his belly, hot and sweet. Brennan fought to keep whatever good sense he had left. Elle felt so good in his arms, as if she'd been shaped to fit against him. Her big brown eyes, usually light, were dark now. Elle wanted him as much as he wanted her.

The knowledge drew a lust-filled groan from deep within his chest. Brennan pulled his mouth from Elle's and struggled to catch his breath. In her flushed face, he saw the effect his kiss had on her.

Elle straightened the red crepe dress she was wearing. "You should go back outside."

Brennan fingered the matching red bolero jacket she wore. "Sweetheart, you really don't have to leave. Charis has nothing to say. She's just trying to make you jealous."

"I know that. I just need a minute to myself and I want to check on my family."

"Are you sure that's all it is?"

"Yes." Elle smiled. "Come join me in a few minutes." Laughing, she added, "If I don't see you in ten minutes, I'm going to come looking for you."

Brennan watched her until she disappeared from sight. As he turned around, his smile vanished. He made his way back to Charis.

A peal of laughter erupted from Charis upon Brennan's return. "Boy, she sure ran out of here. Was it something I said?"

His look was openly hostile. "I want you to turn around and walk out of that door, and don't ever come back. Have I made myself clear?"

"You can't possibly believe this marriage is going to work. She's not your type and all she wants is to drain your bank accounts dry."

Glowering at her, Brennan snapped, "You don't know anything about Elle."

"I don't think you know her as well as you think you do."

With a small twitch of his lips, Brennan said, "Charis, do me a big favor and leave. I don't want this evening ruined for Elle."

Charis gave him an angry glare. *"Forget it, Brennan.* I intend to stay here for the announcement. I want to hear you say that you intend to marry Miss Ransom. Who knows? I may even make an announcement of my own." She threw the words at him like stones.

Frowning, he asked, "What do you have to announce? Are you getting married, too?"

She laughed. "You'll just have to wait and see."

"Charis, it's so good to see you," Elizabeth said gaily as she joined them. "I'm so happy you could make it. Brennan, doesn't she look stunning?"

He sensed more behind his mother's baiting than usual. The lively twinkle in her eyes only incensed him more. *This was all her doing.* Brennan vowed to confront her after the party ended. How dare she interfere with his life? He was furious and didn't care if she knew it.

"Well, isn't she?" Elizabeth prompted.

Brennan regarded his mother and Charis with a lifted brow. Without a word, he stormed off.

Charis burst into laughter.

Looking back at her, Elizabeth asked, "What could possibly be so funny?"

"Before the night is over, Brennan will be mine and Elle Ransom will be an unpleasant memory."

"He says she's carrying his child."

Shrugging, Charis said, "Just leave everything to me, Mrs. Cunningham. I've given you my word. After tonight, Elle won't want to have anything to do with Brennan."

"I hope you're right." Elizabeth fingered the double strand of pearls draped around her neck. "I must get back to my guests."

Charis's smile vanished. "For your sake, Elizabeth, you'd better pray that our little plan works." She waited a moment before following.

Chapter Six

"Who is that woman?" Jillian asked in a low whisper.

"Someone from Brennan's past," Elle whispered back. "Her name is Charis Wentworth. She and Brennan were an item for almost three years. They broke up about two years ago. I think she's been living in Hawaii since then."

"What's she doing here now?"

Shrugging, Elle answered, "Who really knows?" Deep down, she was wondering that very same thing. Why had Charis suddenly come back? Was it just to break them up? If so, she was going to be disappointed.

"Elle, are you sure you know what you're getting into? The last thing you need right now is a lot of drama. It's not good for you or the baby."

"I'm fine," she lied. Elle's stomach churned with anxiety. She was already nervous over the event itself, but Brennan's ex-girlfriend showing up out of the blue like this made her very uneasy.

"Excuse me," a woman softly interjected. "I wanted

to introduce myself. I'm Muffin Worthington, a close friend of the Cunninghams.''

Wearing a simple black sheath dress adorned with a double strand of creamy pearls, with thick chin-length hair that was beautifully styled, revealing tasteful pearl earrings, Muffin appeared very cultured and at ease in her surroundings.

''It's very nice to meet you, Miss Worthington. I've heard Brennan speak of you often. This is my sister, Jillian Sanders.''

As the two women talked, Elle quietly observed Muffin, one of the women Brennan absolutely adored. Her first impression was that Muffin was very gentle, yet hidden in her gentleness was a sense of cleverness and wisdom.

''Dear, I'm so happy for you and Brennan.'' Muffin's smile was honest and sincere, her warmness easing away Elle's discomfort.

''Thank you,'' she murmured.

''We must get together very soon.''

She and Elle talked for a few minutes more before Muffin walked away.

''She seems nice enough,'' Jillian observed.

''Yes, she does,'' Elle agreed. ''I think I'm going to like her. I wish Brennan's mother were more like Ms. Worthington.''

Jillian chuckled. ''She is quite stuffy. I think if she cracked a real smile, the poor woman would break in two.''

Smiling, Elle pinched her sister. ''Be nice.'' Unable to help herself, she burst into laughter.

Arm in arm, she and Jillian strolled over to where the rest of the family was seated.

''Are you all having a good time?'' Elle asked.

"It's okay," Ray answered. "When we leave here, I'm going to stop and pick up something to eat, though."

She was confused. "You haven't eaten? There's plenty of food here."

"Nothing I recognize." Frowning, Ray stated, "I had a couple of those finger sandwiches, and to tell you the truth, I don't know if it was chicken salad or tuna. I decided to leave the rest of it alone."

Everyone burst into laughter.

"You're terrible, Ray," Carrie admonished her husband.

"You didn't know, either. You asked me."

Regis tapped Elle on the arm. "I think Brennan's looking for you."

She glanced over her shoulder. He was coming her way. "I'll talk to you all in a bit." Elle rushed to meet him. "So, what was so important that Charis had to crash our engagement party?"

"Charis had nothing to say, but I knew that already." Brennan took Elle's hand. "Let's get something to eat."

Seated at the table a few minutes later, she had to agree with her brother. She didn't know if she was eating chicken or tuna. It wasn't bad, though.

Pookie ambled over to their table with a man who looked to be around Elle's age in tow.

"Hello, my darlings. I'm so sorry I'm late."

Upon closer inspection, Elle could tell that Pookie was a little breathless and looked a little rumpled. She grinned knowingly.

Stroking the man's arm, Pookie said, "Arthur and I needed to get reacquainted. He's been away for a month."

"You don't need to say more," Brennan announced quickly.

Elle laughed.

Gesturing to the empty chairs at their table, he said, "Why don't you two join us?"

Arthur pulled out a chair for Pookie, who gracefully slid into it. "Thank you, sugar." Signaling for the waiter, she stated, "I'm parched. I need a glass of champagne."

The waiter arrived to take the drink orders.

Turning to face Elle, Pookie smiled. "I'm so excited about the wedding. It's going to be so much fun."

"I'll be glad when it's over," Elle confessed. "It's hard work planning a wedding. I don't know why my sister loves this line of work."

"She's probably a romantic at heart like me."

Nodding, Elle said, "That's Kaitlin. She loves weddings."

The waiter returned, carrying a tray of drinks.

Elle stole a peek at Brennan. "Why are you so quiet all of a sudden?"

He smiled at her. "I was just trying to figure out why Charis suddenly decided to show up after all this time."

"Charis is here?" Pookie questioned.

Brennan nodded. "Yes. She says that she may even make some sort of announcement tonight."

"About what?" Elle and Pookie inquired in unison.

"I don't know."

"Well, maybe the wench has found a fool to marry her," Pookie stated. "I sure pity the poor man."

Brennan agreed. "That's what I was thinking, too."

Elle didn't think so. She didn't know why, but she had a bad feeling about the woman. She was pretty sure that the only man Charis wanted to marry was Brennan. Elle couldn't help but ponder just how far Charis Wentworth would go to make that happen.

* * *

Charis seethed with mounting rage as she watched Brennan and Elle laughing and talking.

"I intend to have Brennan, so you might as well face it, Elle Ransom. I will not be left empty-handed. *Not this time,*" she whispered.

Pushing away from the table, Charis rose to her feet. It was time to put the first part of her plan into action. Her gaze met Elizabeth's and held.

Brushing her hair away from her face, Charis made her way to the stage. She picked up a microphone and gestured for the band to stop playing. "Hello, everyone. How's everybody doing tonight?"

Not waiting for a response, Charis continued on. "This is an announcement party, and I have a little news to share."

She smiled at the look of confusion on Brennan's face. His entire world was about to change. Charis had a definite gleam of triumph in her eyes as she spoke. "Two years ago, when I left for Hawaii, I took a little secret with me. I was pregnant." She paused for effect. "Thirteen months ago, Brennan and I became parents to a beautiful little girl."

Shocked, Elle looked up at him, her eyes filling with tears. "Brennan, did you kn-know about th-this?" The shock caused the words to wedge themselves in her throat. She stared wordlessly at him.

He just sat there, blank, amazed, and very shaken.

"Charis never told you once that she was carrying your child?"

Brennan shook his head in denial. "I'm just as shocked as you are. I don't believe this."

Ray interrupted them.

She hadn't heard him come up. Before Elle could get a word out, he said, "I've tried to stay out of your business, sis, but it's time Brennan and I had a little talk."

"No. This is between us. Stay out of it, Ray."

Brennan stood up. "Elle, it's fine with me. If your brother has something to say to me—then let him. We'll be back shortly."

"Where are you going?" Elle demanded to know. Rising up, she asked, "Why can't you talk here?"

Ray embraced her. "Honey, we're just going to talk. I promise. There's no need to worry."

Fighting tears, Elle sank down into her chair. This was not going well at all. Maybe it was a sign. Maybe marriage just wasn't in their future.

She spied Charis coming toward her table. Elle itched to knock the smug look off her face, but resolved to keep her expression blank.

"Where's Brennan?" Charis asked sweetly. "We need to talk."

"He's with my brother. They should be back in a few minutes."

"Elle—" Charis began but was interrupted by Elizabeth.

"Dear, how could you keep something like this to yourself?" she questioned. "Brennan never would have left your side had he known."

Elle didn't believe Elizabeth Cunningham's act for one minute. She even had her doubts about whether this was the first time she'd heard about the child.

"I'm sure this comes as quite a shock to you," Elizabeth said to Elle.

"Yes, I admit that this is a shock to me. What about you?"

Elizabeth appeared a little taken aback by Elle's question. "Of course. I'm as surprised as you are."

Somehow, I really doubt that, Elle thought, but she kept her feelings under wraps.

Ray's medium brown eyes clawed him like talons. "How could you involve my sister in this mess?"

Brennan met Ray's gaze straight on. "I didn't know anything about Charis being pregnant. This is news to me as well."

"I think you need to leave Elle alone."

"I'm going to marry your sister," Brennan replied sharply. "She's carrying my child."

"And what about this other child? You certainly can't marry both women."

Brennan scoffed at the idea. "I have no intention of marrying Charis. If the child proves to be mine, I'll move forward from there. But right now, I intend to make sure that Elle is okay." He rushed off.

Spotting his mother across the room, Brennan headed purposefully in her direction. "You knew about the baby?" he accused. "How could you not tell me about the child?"

Elizabeth wore a mask of innocence. "I didn't know about any of this, Brennan. This has come as a shock to me as well."

"I don't believe you, Mother."

"I swear to you. I didn't know about the baby." Elizabeth reached out for him, but Brennan stepped away.

Lowering her voice, she asked, "Do you love Elle Ransom?"

Her question drew him to a halt. "I care for her."

Yes, Elle meant something—just what that something was, Brennan didn't care to admit. How could she get to him when no other woman had ever gotten to him at all?

His mother's voice cut into his musings. "Son, if you do not love this girl—why marry her?"

"Mother, you're a strange one to talk. You and Father married for business reasons. He wanted to merge Cunningham Cosmetics with Lake Fragrances."

Elizabeth paled. "Who on earth told you that?"

"Pookie. So don't bother denying it. Besides, it was a smart business decision. My father and my uncle became partners and now hold one of the two biggest cosmetic companies in the world."

"Your father and I care for each other. We are good friends."

"I believe that much is true. But I didn't fail to notice you never mentioned the word 'love'."

"Son, I know this news of a child comes as a shock to you—"

"I need to find my fiancée." Brennan walked away.

"Can you believe this?" Ivy sniped. "These rich people are nuts. They really don't care who they hurt."

"Can't you be just a little more sensitive? Elle is in trouble right now," Kaitlin snapped. "She needs us."

"Whose side do you think I'm on? I was just saying that Elle is better off without Brennan. Rich people have lots of problems to go with all that money. Our sister doesn't need to get caught up in the madness."

"Elle is a grown woman. She'll decide what's best for her. Just leave her be."

"But, Mama . . ."

Amanda laid a gentle hand on Ivy's arm. "This is your sister's life. We will support her no matter what she decides."

Sighing in resignation, Ivy nodded.

Brennan eased up beside Elle, putting a halt to their conversation. "I hate to break this up, but I really need to talk to my fiancée."

Kaitlin turned to her sister. "Do you want to talk to him, Elle? You don't have to."

"I want to do this."

When they were alone, Brennan pulled Elle into his arms. "I'm so sorry about this."

She took a step back from him. Folding her arms across her chest, she stated, "I guess you're as much of a victim in this as I am."

"I didn't know she was pregnant. We took precautions . . ." His voice died.

"Nothing is foolproof. We were careful, too, remember?"

"I know that." Brennan reached out, stroking her cheek. "Elle, I still want to marry you."

"You told me that you won't have our child a bastard. What about your daughter? What do you plan to do about her?"

Pookie interrupted them. It was clear to Elle that she was furious.

"I hope you're planning to have a paternity test performed before you start proclaiming yourself father of a child we haven't seen," Pookie stated flatly. "I, for one, don't trust that Cunningham wanna-be."

"I haven't really thought anything out that far. Outside of marrying Elle."

"So, you two are still planning to marry? I'm so pleased." Pookie reached out, stroking Elle's shoulder. "Don't you worry your pretty little head about any of this. Brennan will get this mess all straightened out. You just stand by your man. That's all you need to do."

Nodding, Elle allowed Brennan to lead her over to a secluded area.

"Will you leave with me right now? We can get on my plane and get married somewhere far from here."

Her body stiffened in shock. "You want to elope?"

"Yes. I need to get away from all the craziness. I'll make a call and we can leave within the hour."

"I need to pack," Elle mumbled. She took a quick breath of utter astonishment.

"We don't have time. We'll buy whatever we need when we get to where we're going."

"Where is that?"

"Let's just get out of here first."

Hand in hand, Brennan and Elle made their way toward the door. Just before they could make their escape, they were halted by a male voice.

A smile lit up Brennan's face. "You made it!" The two men embraced.

The handsome man nodded. "Just got in. Is this your lovely bride-to-be?"

Elle stared at the two men. They could almost be brothers, they looked so much alike, but she knew Brennan was an only child.

"Honey, this is my cousin, Randall Lake. You met his sister, Jordan, earlier."

She smiled. "It's a pleasure to meet you, Randall."

"My cousin's struck gold, I see. Welcome to the family." He embraced her.

Randall glanced around. "What's all the buzzing about?"

"It seems that I have a daughter."

He glanced from Brennan to Elle. "Really? When did you find out?"

"No, Randall. We don't know the sex of the baby Elle's carrying. Charis and I have a daughter together. She just made the announcement. *Here.*"

Randall's mouth dropped open. "You're kidding me! You and Charis have a child together?"

Brennan nodded. "So it seems."

Randall was shaking his head in disbelief.

Taking Elle by the hand once more, Brennan said, "It's good seeing you, Randall. Elle and I are on our way out of here, so I'll catch you later."

"You two are leaving?"

"Yes. Do me a favor and keep Charis occupied."

Randall nodded. "Sure. No problem."

Brennan looked at her and asked, "Ready?"

"You're really serious about this?"

He nodded. "I thought that much was clear."

Elle was a little hesitant. "But my family. I need to tell them something. I can't just leave like this. . . ."

Brennan would not relinquish his hold on her arm. "We'll send them a telegram." Elle was still too astonished by his suggestion that they elope to offer any objections.

Chapter Seven

Looking around the room, Randall finally spotted Charis standing a few feet away. She was being her usual flirtatious self. Walking swiftly, he made his way over to her.

She gave him a pretty smile and promptly excused herself from the circle of adoring men that surrounded her. She held her arms open, saying, "Randall, honey, it's so good to see you." Pouting, she added, "You've been a naughty boy. You never once called me."

"What on earth do you think you're doing?" he demanded. Randall grabbed Charis by the arm none too gently, pulling her off to the side, away from any of the guests. "This is a dangerous game you're playing."

Snatching her arm away, she glared at him. "I'm not playing games. I simply told the truth. Lauren is Brennan's daughter."

"How can you be so sure?"

Charis even had the nerve to look offended. "Because I *know*." She glanced around them furtively. "Please keep your voice lowered. We wouldn't want anyone to get the wrong idea, would we?"

Randall was so disgusted by her at the moment. How could he have ever cared for her? "He's still marrying Elle. Your little surprise did nothing to change the situation."

"Maybe. Maybe not. It's not over, Randall. Not by a long shot."

"Why don't you leave them alone? It's not like you're in love with Brennan."

"You don't have any idea what you're talking about. Of course I love Brennan. He and I belong together."

"I find that so hard to believe. Especially after what happened."

Charis's eyes flashed in anger. "I don't care what you believe. Randall, you may think you know me, but you don't. You misunderstood what happened back then. I was confused at the time. Brennan and I were fighting—"

"Don't you mean he dumped you?"

Her petite body stiffened. "We agreed that it was best if we spent some time apart." Charis laid her hand on his arm. "Randall, you're such a dear to me, but if you get in my way, I'll destroy you. How do you think Brennan would feel if he knew how long you've been lusting after me? Think of all those times he trusted me with you. . . ."

"I don't know what I ever saw in you."

Charis's response was her laughter as she left him standing alone in the corner.

* * *

"Where's Elle?" Jillian asked, as her eyes bounced around the area. "I haven't seen her for a while. Come to think of it, I don't see Brennan, either."

"They must be somewhere talking," Carrie stated. "You have to admit, they do have an awful lot to discuss."

Ivy made a face. "If it were me, there would be no discussion."

"It's easy for *us* to say that," Carrie responded. "We're not in her shoes. Elle loves Brennan."

Sighing, Jillian agreed. "But can love conquer all in this situation?"

"So, where are we headed?" Elle inquired. "It's okay to tell me now. We're on your private plane thousands of miles above the ground. This place is as safe as any." A flash of humor crossed her face. "I almost feel like James Bond."

Laughing, Brennan agreed. "We're going to Eastport, Michigan. We have a beach cottage on Torch Lake."

"Is that where we're getting married?"

"Yes." The warmth of his smile echoed in his voice. "From there we'll head to the Virgin Islands for our honeymoon as planned."

"Why not get married there?"

He shrugged. "I don't know. I guess I chose Torch Lake because it's the place where I've always found peace. I've always felt at home there."

"That's how I feel about going to my mother's house in Riverside." Elle played with her fingers. "So, how are you feeling about all this?"

"What? The marriage?"

She shook her head. "I'm talking about your daughter."

"I'm still in shock. I don't know how I feel about the situation. I'm not going to abandon her."

"I know that. Everything happened so fast, but did you get a chance to talk to Charis?"

"No. I couldn't deal with her at the time. As soon as we return, though, I'm going to have a long talk with her."

Elle agreed. "You two definitely have a lot to discuss."

"You think there's really a baby?"

"Don't you?"

"I don't know. Charis is a big liar."

"I don't know her at all, but I really don't think she'd lie to you about having a child. It's too easy to verify."

"You're right." Brennan leaned back in his seat. "We'll get all this straight after we get back. For now, let's just concentrate on us."

It was well after midnight when the plane landed. They were met by a limo and taken directly to the house.

"Make yourself at home. I need to check on a few things."

Elle nodded. She strolled over to the sofa and sank down. The place was spotless. It was hard to imagine with the home hardly used.

She was watching television when Brennan returned. He sat down beside her. Elle noted his set face, his clamped mouth and fixed eyes. Nervously, she moistened her lips.

Brennan stated, "You haven't said much. Are you okay with this?"

Stretching her legs casually before her, Elle replied, "I wouldn't have come if I wasn't. I'm looking forward to being your wife."

Brennan's mouth twisted wryly. "I'm sorry about Charis. . . ."

"You don't have to apologize," Elle assured him.

"It's not okay, but you won't have to worry about Charis. She's harmless."

"I'm not so sure I agree with you on that." Elle stifled a yawn.

Brennan kissed her on the forehead. "It's late. Why don't you get some sleep?"

"What about you? Aren't you coming?"

"I need to make a few phone calls before I go to bed." Brennan kissed her. "I'll see you in the morning."

"I should call my mother. I don't want her to worry."

"I had Mimi call from the plane. Everything is under control, so go to bed."

Elle sleepily blew him a kiss and made her way to the bedroom. She took off her clothes and took a quick shower.

She had just gotten out when she heard a knock on the door. When she heard Brennan's voice, she wrapped a towel around herself and said, "Come in."

"I had some clothing delivered to the house before we landed. It's in the master bedroom. You should find something there to fit you."

"Thanks."

His grin flashed briefly, dazzling against his smooth, dark chocolate skin. "I told you I would take care of everything. I meant it."

Brennan's voice soothed her and she drank in the comfort of his nervousness. Elle's feelings for him were intensifying, and it scared her. She felt a certain sadness as the hour of their wedding approached.

In less than twenty-four hours, Elle would be marrying

the man she'd waited her whole life for. Only he didn't love her.

As soon as Elle's head hit the soft down pillow, she fell into a dreamless sleep.

The next morning, Elle could not believe her eyes. Timbers cut from behind the beach house created a solid ceremonial focal point at the water's edge. A floral mix of daisies, flax, and Queen Anne's lace was placed in baskets that sat atop the posts.

"You've been busy," she murmured to Brennan.

"Do you like it? I know this isn't what you had in mind when we decided to marry, but I want you to be happy."

Embracing him, she said, "Oh, Brennan, I like it. I really do."

"If you check the master bedroom, you'll find a wedding gown. It's similar to the one you wanted. I also had a silk runner made from the same fabric. At this very moment, I have some men constructing a makeshift floor that will lead from the house to where we'll be standing during the ceremony."

"You're so thoughtful." Elle glanced around. Brennan had gone out of his way to make this day special for her. Even the weather was cooperating. The first day of spring still bore the brisk air of winter, but the day was a beautiful one for a ceremony. If only her family could share in this day with them . . .

"You're thinking about your family," Brennan interjected. "I'm sure you wish they were here."

"It would be nice," Elle admitted. "But right now I'm not going to dwell on it. I need to get ready for our wedding."

"The hairstylist will be arriving soon."

"You've thought of everything, I see." Elle awarded

him with a kiss, then headed back up to the cottage. The next time she saw Brennan, they would be pledging their souls to each other.

Five hours later, with the ocean and the fiery blaze of sunset as their witnesses, Brennan and Elle became man and wife.

When they returned from the waterfront to the cottage, the housekeeper led the newlyweds straight to the formal dining room. In accordance with Brennan's instructions, a white-and-gold color theme prevailed.

The table settings were a balance of high and low with a short, lush arrangement of full-blown roses and tall, thin tapers gracing the marble dining-room table. Plates made of bone china sat on gold chargers and crystal glasses sparkled in the candlelight.

On the antique sideboard, candied roses embellished the wedding cake.

Guiding Elle to a chair, Brennan said, "The chef prepared a special meal for us. Lobster ravioli, Chilean sea bass, and berries brûlée in a sabayon-champagne sauce."

Elle was touched he'd remembered. She loved lobster ravioli. She gave Brennan a tiny smile as she sat down in the chair he held out for her.

Moving around the table, he sat down across from her. A maid appeared out of nowhere with a bottle of champagne. After filling their glasses, she disappeared as quietly as she'd arrived.

Picking up his flute, Brennan said, "Thank you for the honor of being your husband. It's a title I will wear with pride."

In that instance, all of her doubts vanished. Elle smiled. "I'm so glad you said that, because it's the same way I feel."

As soon as they finished dinner, Elle cut into the

bottom tier of the two-tier wedding cake. The two of them shared a slice. Grinning, Elle stuffed the last of the cake into Brennan's mouth.

Icing lingered on his full lips. Leaning forward, he kissed her. When he pulled away, Elle wiped his mouth with a linen napkin, then wiped her own.

There was a long moment of stillness; then in a deep, quiet voice, Brennan said, "Are you ready to go to bed?"

She, too, waited several heartbeats before a breathless "yes" trembled from her lips.

Upstairs, Elle prepared for her wedding night. In the bedroom, she changed into an Italian-lace chemise and kimono robe of pale celery.

Nervous, she eased into the master bedroom, where Brennan lay waiting for her. She heard his sharp intake of breath, but held back her smile. Acutely aware of Brennan watching her, Elle sank down on the plush cushion of the vanity bench. Staring at her reflection in the mirror, she took down her hair.

Brennan glided out of bed. He was wearing a pair of black silk boxers from which Elle couldn't seem to tear her gaze. Even in the mirror, she could see the desire in his eyes.

Standing behind her, Brennan placed his hands on her shoulders, his palms sliding beneath her robe and the slender straps of her gown.

Closing her eyes, Elle leaned back against him. The touch of his fingers in her hair as he gathered it from where it hung past Elle's shoulders made her want things she'd never wanted before.

"You are so beautiful, sweetheart. I will never tire of looking at you." Brennan pulled her up to her feet.

Gazing into her husband's eyes, Elle slid her gown down to bare smooth, mocha-hued skin to him, letting it fall to a shimmering puddle at her feet. In the moonlight, her skin was golden.

A faint smile curved the hard line of Brennan's mouth as he eyed her. In the soft light, Elle could see his reaction to her. She captured his lips with hers once more.

"Elle," he whispered, his voice almost a groan, and he swung her up and into his arms, crossing the room with her to lay her down atop the high bed.

He followed after taking off his boxers. Brennan held her in his arms. His head lowered and he trailed kisses over her throat, neck, and shoulders.

Elle had glimpses of Brennan's broad chest with dark hair curling over it, and a flat, taut stomach with ridges of muscle. Being with him like this made her tingle in response, and Elle felt a wash of love for this man that frightened her.

Although she knew that it was dangerous to love Brennan, she couldn't help herself. Elle couldn't hold back the sweep of response at his touch. Nothing would ever be the same, she thought in a passion-filled haze.

Elle couldn't think anymore as Brennan's kisses, his hands, and his body lifted her up in a swirling vortex of ecstasy.

Did he love her after all? He'd made love to her most of the night. Elle was convinced that Brennan couldn't possibly touch her the way he did without having some sort of feelings for her. Their lovemaking wasn't merely filling a moment of physical desire—it was the tearing apart of her soul in one instance and mending it back together in another.

Maybe Brennan loved her just a little, Elle decided. If so, she would accept it without complaint. But she had to ask herself, would it be enough for them to build a life on?

She woke up to the sound of Brennan singing in the shower the next morning. Brennan had such a beautiful voice. Elle wondered why he'd chosen to give up his career as a recording artist.

"Why did you stop singing?" Elle asked when he came out of the bathroom. "You could probably have legions of fans all over the world by now. Several gold albums and I'd bet a few platinum ones, too."

"I was young. . . ." Brennan sighed. "My father wanted me to join him in the company."

"You left a promising career as a singer for your father?"

He nodded. "I thought it would bring us closer."

"Did it?"

"No."

"Do you miss it? Performing, I mean."

"Sometimes. I think I'd rather work behind the scenes now."

"Why don't you do that?"

"Malcolm and I have talked about it from time to time." Shrugging, Brennan said, "My father always acts as if I'm betraying him when I talk about leaving. But the truth be known, I hate being there. I hate the glorified position I hold."

"I'm sorry. I admire you, though. You are making such a huge sacrifice because you love your father."

Brennan's face grew grim. "This is our honeymoon. I don't want to waste time talking about family. Especially my family." Leaning his head down, he covered her mouth with his, kissing her passionately.

Chapter Eight

"Wake up," Brennan whispered as he shook her gently. He and Elle had spent the last twenty-four hours in bed.

Elle didn't respond.

His hand slid higher, gently cupping her jaw. "Wake up, sweetheart."

She blinked widely as she was roused from a deep sleep. "Good morning," Elle murmured softly.

He laughed. "Honey, it's six-thirty in the evening. Dinner is going to get cold unless we hurry and get dressed."

She instantly became wide awake. "You cooked?"

Brennan shook his head. "Cooking is not a talent I possess."

"Who made dinner?"

"We have a chef in our employ, remember?"

Elle sat up and pushed the covers down, revealing her nakedness. Suddenly feeling self-conscious, she reached for her robe.

Brennan got to it first. "You don't ever have to hide yourself from me. I enjoy looking at you." As their eyes met, he felt a shock run through him.

"I can't believe you're really going to let me out of bed."

"You need your strength," he teased. "You aren't complaining, are you?"

Elle shook her head. "No, not at all." She quickly snatched her robe from him and slipped it on. "When do we leave for St. John?" She headed to the bathroom.

"Early tomorrow morning." Taking off his shirt, Brennan followed her.

Elle stopped beneath the archway. Grinning, she asked, "What do you think you're doing?"

"Taking a shower with you."

She gave him a smile that sent his pulse racing. "I'm taking a bath. I need to soak some of the soreness away."

His brow creased with worry. "Did I hurt you?"

"No," Elle replied. "You didn't hurt me."

"I'm sorry, baby," he murmured softly.

She stroked his cheek. "I'm okay. It's nothing to be sorry over. I wanted you as much as you wanted me."

He turned on the water in the garden tub. "Enjoy your bath. I'll have Raul keep dinner warm."

Elle looked at him in surprise. "You're not going to join me in the tub?"

Brennan's mouth twisted wryly. "Do you want me to?"

She removed her robe in answer.

"This is so unlike Elle," Amanda stated. "What in the world has gotten into the girl? First she runs off without telling anyone, and then we get a phone call from one of Brennan's employees.''

"Humph. I don't think you really want to know," Ivy threw in, her mouth thinning with displeasure.

"Need I remind everyone that Elle is a grown woman?" Jillian pointed out. "She and Brennan will be married in a couple of weeks anyway. There's nothing wrong with them getting away for a few days. I don't blame them."

"This just arrived. It's a telegram," Laine announced.

Amanda read the note. "We can forget about the wedding." Her faint smile held a touch of sadness.

"Did they break up?" Ivy asked hopefully. "It's about time Elle came to her senses."

"Elle didn't break up with Brennan. They eloped."

Jillian gasped. "Elle ran off and married him after all. I guess I'm not that surprised. She really loved this man."

"Well, I'm not so sure I like him," Allura announced. "Now he's part of our family. We're stuck with him for the time being."

"Yes, we are," Amanda agreed. "And when they return, all of you will treat Brennan Cunningham as family."

Ray's face grew grim. "Mom, this is going to be hard. Elle's sweet and shy. She's not ready to take on that arrogant . . ."

"Your sister made a choice, son." Amanda took a deep breath, her expression tight with strain. "If Elle's made her bed hard—she'll be the one to lie in it."

Jillian's face was as glum as those of her siblings. "Hmmmm . . . I wonder how the Cunninghams are taking the news. They weren't exactly thrilled about Elle marrying Brennan in the first place."

"You've got to admit that none of us are happy about the marriage, either," Laine confessed.

"I just pray Elle won't have to pay with her heart." Ivy folded her arms across her chest. "She's always been the sensitive one. I'll break his neck if he hurts my sister."

Carrie spoke up. "I'm going to think positive. She's a Ransom. Elle will bring Brennan to his knees. Just watch."

Amanda gave her a concerned glance. "Dear heart, I pray that you're right. Lord knows I do."

"Has anyone heard from Brennan?" Charis asked. "I'm so worried about him. Maybe I should fly up to Torch Lake. Lauren and I could join him there." She smiled, clearly pleased with her idea. "Actually, that's not a bad plan. It would be the perfect place for us to reunite as a family."

"I bet," Pookie commented.

Elizabeth handed Charis a glass of juice. "Maybe he just needed to get away alone to deal with the shock. I'm sure we'll hear from him soon. Brennan always runs off to Torch Lake when he needs to think things over. It's his home away from home."

Belle eased into the room. "This just arrived by messenger." She handed a yellow envelope to Elizabeth, who promptly read it.

"Oh, dear Lord!" The paper fluttered to the floor.

Charis dived after the letter. She read it quickly. *"He married her. Brennan married Elle Ransom."*

Pookie released a loud yelp. "That's my boy. I'm so happy for him."

Charis frowned with cold fury.

"How could he be such a fool?" Elizabeth muttered. She pulled on the sleeves of her dress. "Brennan has no idea what he's done. Was there even a prenuptial agreement?"

"What for?" Pookie asked.

Shaking her head, Elizabeth said, "This marriage isn't going to work."

"How do you know?"

Elizabeth turned to her sister, her face a marble mask of anger. "Pookie, my son should have made this woman sign a prenuptial. He should have been smarter about this."

"The boy's in love."

"He is not in love with Elle," Charis argued. "I'm sure it was all her idea. She panicked and took advantage of Brennan's vulnerability. That's all it was."

Pookie's expression held a note of mockery. "You'd love to believe that, wouldn't you?" She laughed as she strolled toward the door. With a slight wave of her hand, Pookie said, "I'll see you two later. I've got some serious man shopping to do. I need a date for Friday night."

"You're disgusting," Elizabeth uttered.

"You just hate me because I'm cute. I can't help it though, so you might as well accept it." Pulling out her cell phone, Pookie punched in a number.

Once they were the only two in the room, Charis inclined her head and said, "I guess this changes things, doesn't it, Elizabeth?"

They stared at each other across a sudden ringing silence.

Elizabeth's gray eyes darkened as she held Charis's gaze. "It certainly does not, my dear. If you play your hand intelligently, you can still have my son."

Charis frowned in exasperation. "He married Elle

Ransom. How can you be so convinced he doesn't love her?"

Her brittle smile softened slightly. "It's my gut feeling."

"She's also pregnant." Charis's expression grew hard and resentful.

"It's unfortunate on her part. I'm sure Brennan will allow generous visitation rights."

Charis frowned. "I don't want her brat hanging around us. Let Elle keep her own child. I'm certainly not going to raise it."

"That will be for you and Brennan to decide. Just do all that you can to break them up." Elizabeth evaluated her with a critical squint. "If you fail, you and Lauren will lose everything. *Remember that.*"

"I think you have that wrong, Elizabeth. It's you who will lose."

There was derision in Elizabeth's gaze. "Do not make the mistake of believing that particular fact." She kept her features deceptively composed. "You do not want to make an enemy of me, Charis." Her mouth spreading into a thin-lipped smile, Elizabeth added, "I don't expect to see you again until after Brennan returns. I've tolerated your presence as much as I can for now."

Elizabeth started to walk away, then stopped. "Oh, and dear, you may want to fly your nanny and the child here. It would at least give the appearance that you are a caring mother." Elizabeth's tone was coolly disapproving.

Charis couldn't control the spasmodic trembling within her. Fury almost choked her. Clenching her fists, she fought to keep her temper under wraps. She could not afford to yield to the anger and bitterness that burned within.

Charis glanced sharply around, her eyes blazing. One way or another, all this was going to be hers. She had grown up in the lap of luxury, and since her father's death and the enormous amount of debt he'd left, Charis had to ensure that her future would be a financially secure one.

Chapter Nine

Brennan and Elle arrived on the island of St. John and were taken by car to an elegant villa about four miles from Cruz Bay. Elle fell in love with the blend of creamy pink stucco walls surrounded by an abundance of tropical plants and flowers. The villa was nestled high above the bay with a stunning view of the island of St. Croix in the distance.

She trembled with excitement as Brennan gave her a tour of the villa. The great room was a unique hexagonal shape with high ceilings and oversize mahogany doors that opened onto the terrace. The villa also featured a thirty-foot swimming pool with a shaded gazebo.

Elle turned to face her husband. "This place is great! Like some wonderful romantic dream." She smiled. "I'm in no hurry to wake up."

"I'm glad you're happy. Especially here. This will be our home for the next four weeks."

Her mouth dropped open. "We're going to be here for a month? Why so long?"

"It's our honeymoon, and I want to take this time for us." Slowly and seductively, Brennan's gaze slid downward. "*Just us.*"

"Well, I'm not going to complain. I'm going to take advantage of the time I have with you. I know how much you travel on business."

"You travel quite a bit yourself. I'm hoping you're going to start slowing down. You're almost four and a half months pregnant."

Placing her hand over his mouth, Elle laughed. "We're on our honeymoon. Let's not talk about jobs right now. They will be there when we get back."

. Elle was thrilled to have this time alone with Brennan, but she had never been away from her family for that long of a period. She was really going to miss them.

Later that evening, she broke down and called her mother while Brennan was in the shower.

"It's so good to hear from you, baby."

"I'm sorry I haven't called before now. I just didn't quite know what to say."

"I understand. Elle, you know all I care about is your happiness."

"I am happy, Mama." Hearing Brennan singing in the shower, she smiled. "Very happy."

"Then that's all that matters to me. Congratulations on your marriage."

"Brennan is a good man, Mama. He really is. You just have to get to know him."

"I will, baby. When are you coming home?"

"In a month. We're on the island of St. John. It's so beautiful here."

"Take lots of pictures for me."

"I will." Elle was quiet for a moment.

"Honey, you still there?"

"I'm here."

The shower stopped in the bathroom.

"I love you, Mama. I'll see you in about a month, okay?"

"I love you, too, baby. I wish you all the happiness in the world. You deserve nothing less."

Elle hung up the phone just as Brennan glided into the room. She quickly wiped away her tears and smiled. "I just got off the phone with my mother. She sends her best."

"That's nice. I hope she isn't too disappointed in not having a wedding. We can still have one if you want."

Shaking her head, Elle replied, "No, it's not necessary. We're already married. That's enough for me."

"Aren't you like all other little girls? They dream of big beautiful and romantic weddings. It's almost as if they measure love by the size of the wedding and reception."

"If that's true, then we're in big trouble." Elle laughed at the expression on Brennan's face. "I'm only kidding. To answer your question, I would have loved a nice wedding, but it's not necessary. Not having a big fancy wedding doesn't make me any less married."

"You are quite an unusual woman."

"I don't know about all that. I'm sure there are a lot of other women out there who think the way I do." Elle gasped.

"What's wrong?"

"It's the baby. I felt the baby move."

"Is this the first time?"

"I've been feeling tiny little flutters here and there, but this time it felt like a thump."

Brennan burst into laughter.

"It did." Elle reached over, took his hand, and

pressed it against her belly. "Did you feel that one?" she asked.

"I don't feel a thing." Squeezing her hand, Brennan smiled. "I think you're going to be a wonderful mother."

"You really think so?"

He nodded. "Our little one is very lucky to have you as a mother."

Elle gave a small laugh. "Make sure you tell him or her that."

The weeks came and left but not quite fast enough for Elle. She was homesick, and she really missed her family.

That morning Brennan announced that they were going swimming. Although Elle really wasn't in the mood, she was determined to appease her husband by doing what he wanted.

Elle tried on swimsuit after swimsuit, but the result was the same. She wasn't crazy about any of them. She finally decided on the solid black one with the shirred bust. Over it she wore a long ankle-length gauze cover-up.

Brennan looked up from the newspaper he'd been reading and smiled. "You look as beautiful as ever," he said.

"You always seem to know what I need to hear."

Placing a gentle hand on the tiny mound of her stomach, he said, "You're starting to get a belly." Brennan's gaze grew tender. "I can't wait to meet this little person. I'm already impressed by the mother. . . ."

I already love the father, she whispered in her heart.

"Let's get that swim, shall we?"

Elle nodded and took Brennan's hand. They left the house and went out into the April sunshine, stopping long enough for Elle to grab a pair of sunglasses.

The newlyweds spent the afternoon swimming until one of the maids came out carrying a tray of food. She left but quickly returned with drinks.

Brennan climbed out of the pool. Elle climbed out behind him and made her way over to one of the tables.

After a filling and delicious lunch, Brennan jumped back into the pool for one last lap while Elle relaxed on one of the lounge chairs.

It felt so right being in this tropical paradise with Brennan, she mused silently. Ivy was wrong—their marriage was going to last. Elle vowed to do everything in her power to make it work.

Later that evening, Brennan and Elle decided to retire early. Curled up next to him, she watched the play of emotions on her husband's face. She had a feeling she knew exactly what he was thinking about. "You're thinking about her."

Although Brennan knew full well whom Elle was referring to, he asked, "Who are you talking about?"

"Your daughter. Do you want to talk about her? She's not going to go away."

He shrugged. "I really don't know what to say. Never in a million years did I suspect . . . I never thought Charis and I would share a child." Brennan leaned forward, his arms resting on his knees. "I'm going to have a paternity test performed."

"You don't believe Charis is telling the truth?" Elle questioned.

"Charis is . . . well, how can I best explain it? She's

not exactly the mother type. In fact, she never really wanted children. I just want to be sure this is not some sort of prank. If the child is mine, I want custody of her."

Elle was appalled. "You want to take her baby from her?" She shook her head. "Brennan, you can't do that."

"Why not?"

"Because Charis is her mother, and the little girl's been with her since birth. She doesn't know you." She stroked his cheek lovingly. "Right now you're confused and a little angry."

"I'm very angry. I should've known about the child much sooner."

Elle remained quiet. Just a few weeks ago, he hadn't known about her pregnancy, either.

Brennan glanced over at her and patted her knee. "This is not about you and me. We're past that, sweetheart. Besides, I understand why you did what you did. I hurt you."

"It still wasn't right. I admit that. Perhaps Charis felt the same way. I'm sure she was affected by your breakup."

"I think the problem I have with all this is the fact that the child is over a year old. She didn't bother me until now. Why did Charis feel the need to tell me all of a sudden?"

Elle broke into laughter. "Oh, that's easy. You were getting married to another woman. She had probably always assumed you would eventually come after her."

"It's just not making any sense. If you and I hadn't been engaged, would she have ever said anything?"

"I don't know," Elle admitted honestly. "You won't

get any answers here, honey. Maybe we should cut our honeymoon short and go home."

"You're ready to leave?"

"Yes and no. However, I don't think we can really enjoy ourselves with you thinking about Charis and the baby."

"I think about our child as well."

"I know that. Brennan, I'm not feeling insecure about any of this. You didn't have to marry me after you found out. I'm assuming you did because you wanted me to be your wife."

"We'll stay here for another week and then we'll fly home."

"I loved St. John, but I am glad to be home," Elle confessed. Rubbing his shoulder, she added, "I especially loved having you all to myself."

"I had a good time, too."

While Brennan made a few business calls, Elle laid down to take a nap. These days she seemed to tire more easily, and the flight home had worn her out. She was exhausted.

When Elle came downstairs an hour later, she found Brennan in the media room, listening to jazz. She eased down onto the leather couch beside him.

"How was your nap?" he asked.

"Good. I really needed to rest." Nudging him playfully, she teased, "It's probably the most sleep I've gotten since we got married."

Leaning back, Elle opened the book she'd brought downstairs with her. She hadn't been reading long when Brennan announced, "I'll give Malcolm a call later and tell him that he's going to need a new publicist."

Laying down her novel, Elle questioned, "Why would you do that?"

"I've given this a lot of thought. I know how much you love your job, but I would prefer you stay home with our child."

Irritated, Elle sat up straight. "Brennan, this is something we need to talk about. I'm not interested in quitting my job."

"Why not?" he wanted to know.

"As you already know, I love my job. I'd planned on taking off a few months for the baby and then cutting back on my hours, but I'm not quitting."

"We have more than enough money—"

"It's not about the money," Elle interrupted him. "I really love what I do. I'll even donate my salary, but I want to work."

"You love your job that much?"

"Yes, I do."

"I don't want your work coming before our child, Elle. This is something I feel very strongly about."

"I won't let that happen. I will do a lot of work from home—Malcolm and I have already talked about it."

"I'm not crazy about this, but we'll try it out," he said somewhat gruffly. "I guess you're going to need an office." Brennan stood up. "Come with me. I'll show you where you can set up shop."

Elle followed him down the hall to the last room on the left.

"You can use this room as your office. It's already equipped with two separate phone lines. My study is next door."

Glancing around the empty room, Elle murmured, "Thank you."

Brennan took her back upstairs for a complete tour

of the house. In all the time she'd known him, Elle had not seen every room in the house. Most of their time together had been spent at her house.

Three of the bedrooms had private baths and balconies, while the other two shared an adjoining bathroom. The spacious master bed and bath suite had its own sitting room. When Brennan opened a connecting door, Elle glimpsed a nursery.

"The baby will sleep in here," he was saying. "There's also another bathroom on the other side of this room."

"This house is so big. Why did you buy it?"

"I intended to have a family one day." He smiled. "You seem surprised."

"I am. I kind of figured you for a bachelor."

Brennan shook his head. "No. I want nothing to do with love, but I've always wanted a family."

"I see."

"Why don't you make yourself comfortable? I'll have something light sent up for lunch."

"I don't mind preparing myself something to eat. I'm used to it actually."

"Elle, we have a live-in housekeeper and a cook."

"I'm used to taking care of myself. Melina has this entire house to worry about—and on top of that, I can cook for myself. Nobody needs to fix lunch for me."

"I pay these people good money. I intend for them to earn every single penny."

"I realize this. However, I'm not used to having someone else tend to my every need."

"So you want me to send this cute little couple out into the land of the unemployed."

"Well, no . . . now you're making me feel bad."

"It was not my intention. I hired Robert and his wife because I can't properly clean a house and my cooking is even worse. This house is much too big for you to handle on your own. Besides, when you have the baby, your hands are going to be full with trying to balance motherhood and work. Then there's me . . ."

Grinning, Elle said, "Don't worry, I won't neglect you or the baby. If it becomes too much, I'll let you know."

The doorbell sounded.

Elle glanced over at Brennan. "Are you expecting company?"

"No."

When the housekeeper announced their visitor, Elle's mouth twisted into a frown. This was not how she'd envisioned their first night home.

Charis strolled into the room carrying a little girl.

"What are you doing here?" Brennan asked gruffly. "Elle and I just arrived home today."

"I know. When your mother told me you were coming home, I thought it would be the perfect time for Lauren to meet her father." She pulled on the little girl's frilly dress. "It's time you two met, don't you think?"

"Couldn't you have given us a day or so?"

Charis tried to look offended. "Are you saying you don't want to meet your daughter?" She placed a hand over Lauren's ear, drawing anger from Elle.

"You know that's not what he's saying, Charis."

Kissing the toddler's forehead, she sighed dramatically. "Honey, I guess Daddy's too busy for you today. . . ."

"Don't tell her that," Brennan demanded.

"Calm down," Elle advised in a low whisper. "You don't want to scare Lauren."

"I'm sorry. I didn't mean to snap."

Smiling, Charis said, "That's better." Walking over

to Brennan, she held out the little girl to him. "Take your daughter."

He did as he was told.

Fuming, Elle took a seat as Brennan stared at the toddler in awe. Lauren looked every bit like her dad. There was no denying the fact that Brennan had indeed fathered the little girl.

Brennan thought he detected a flash of pain in Elle's expression. She wasn't comfortable with their situation. Here he was bouncing his firstborn on his knee—just a few weeks ago, they'd assumed Elle was carrying his first child.

Charis snaked an arm around him. "Isn't she the most beautiful baby in the world?" she gushed.

His gaze met Elle's. Brennan strolled over to where his new wife was sitting. He sat down on the arm of the chair and held out the little girl to her.

Smiling, Elle took the baby in her arms. "She's adorable, Brennan."

He didn't miss Charis's frustrated sigh, but decided to ignore it. He watched as Elle played with Lauren.

"You are just the sweetest little girl, aren't you?"

The baby grinned.

Charis apparently couldn't stand it anymore. She stalked over and picked up Lauren without preamble. "Come here, sweetie pie. Mommy brought you over here to see your daddy."

Brennan's nostrils flared in anger and he was about to say something, but Elle stilled him by softly stroking his hand. When he glanced over at her, she shook her head.

"I'm sure you are itching to get back to your wife,

but we really need to talk." Staring pointedly at Elle, she added, "Just the two of us."

"What's the hurry, Charis? You took your time telling me I even had a daughter."

"I'll explain all of that to you." The little girl started to squirm. Charis let her slide down to the floor.

Elle rose. "I'm going upstairs. Let me know when she's gone." Without another word, she left the room. Elle was as anxious to go as Charis was for her to leave. The woman brought out the worst in her.

Chapter Ten

Elle left the office early because of a severe headache. As soon as she arrived home, Melina made a fuss over her by sending Elle straight to bed and putting in a call to her doctor.

When Brennan arrived three hours later, he found Elle still in bed and sleeping soundly. He went back downstairs to speak with the housekeeper. He found Melina in the kitchen with her husband.

"Mrs. Cunningham was complaining of a terrible headache. She hasn't looked like herself these past couple of days," Melina explained. "The doctor said it was okay for her to take Tylenol."

"Has she eaten anything?" Brennan inquired.

"No. She didn't want anything."

Brennan turned to Robert. "Will you prepare a pot of your famous chicken soup and a sandwich? I know she loves ham and cheese. I'll see that Elle eats."

Robert smiled and nodded.

Brennan went back upstairs. He took pains to keep

from disturbing his wife, but Elle was already beginning to stir. To him, her face looked a little puffy.

Yawning, she sat up in bed. "When did you get home?"

"Not too long ago. How are you feeling? Still have your headache?"

"A little, but it's not as bad as it was." Elle climbed out of bed.

"Melina's going to bring up something for you to eat. I want you to stay in bed and get some much-needed rest. No more traveling until after the baby's born, Elle." His tone was firm; he brooked no argument. "I'm not going to change my mind on this."

Nodding, Elle agreed. "I'll do it your way," she said in resignation.

Brennan smiled in gratitude.

A week later, she went to see her doctor. She was five and a half months pregnant, and it was time for her regular prenatal visit. For Elle, it turned into a nightmare.

Her doctor was checking for a heartbeat. A strange expression on his face, he looked up at Elle. "Have you felt the baby move in the last eight hours?"

She thought back. "I felt him move last night, but since then . . ." Her voice died and fear raged through her. "Is something wrong?"

The next few minutes were a blur for Elle. She was immediately taken via ambulance to the hospital, where the doctor performed an emergency cesarean.

Brennan arrived just as she was being wheeled from the operating room to recovery. Elle was vaguely aware of him holding her hand. She thought he might have been talking to her, but she couldn't make out the words. There was a drug-induced fog clouding her brain.

When Elle woke up, she found Brennan staring out of the hospital window. She called out weakly, "The baby . . ."

He turned around and walked over to the bed, his face filled with anguish. Brushing the hair from her face with gentle strokes, he whispered, "Sweetheart, take it easy."

Ignoring the pain that ravaged her body, she held out her hand to him. "My baby?"

Brennan's eyes were bright with unshed tears. Without him uttering a word, Elle knew what was coming. The denial came out in a mournful cry. "Nooooo . . ."

A warm, strong hand clasped hers, and Brennan's deep voice said, "Honey, the baby . . . our son didn't survive."

The doctor's office, his words—it all came back to her. Elle started to cry.

"I'm so sorry, sweetheart. If I could change this situation, I would. *I would.*"

Her throat closed over his words and the tears streamed down her face. All the separate hurting dissolved into one tremendous pain that settled around her heart. Elle put her hands to her face, sobbing loudly.

A nurse ventured over.

"We're going to move her to a private room."

Brennan nodded solemnly. He followed as they wheeled her bed down the long corridor to her room.

She hurt all over, it seemed. Elle was in excruciating pain from the C-section, but it didn't come close to the pain in her heart. Her baby was dead. Over and over in her head was the question, *What did I do wrong?*

Awkwardly Brennan sat on the edge of the bed. There was a soft knock on the door. Amanda peeked inside.

Brennan gestured for her to enter. "Your mother's here, sweetheart." He rose to allow Amanda to get closer to the bed, then strolled over to the window once more.

"Baby, I'm so sorry," Amanda said as she stroked Elle's cheek, wiping away her tears.

"Why?" Elle whispered.

"I don't know, baby girl. I just don't know."

Elle recalled trying to console Jillian once after she'd had her first miscarriage. She'd told her sister that it was nature's way of keeping her from having a deformed baby. Now, after her own loss, Elle intended to apologize to her sister, because it meant nothing. The very words meant nothing at all.

A different nurse eased into the room. After giving her condolences, she asked, "Would you like to hold your baby?"

Elle looked over at Brennan and nodded.

Amanda helped her sit up as much as her sore body would allow. Brennan eased down beside her.

The nurse returned carrying a tiny infant wrapped in a blanket. She handed the baby to Elle. Weighing one pound, he fit perfectly in the palm of her hand.

Tears slipping from her eyes, she stared at her son. "He looks just like he's sleeping." A sob caught in her throat. "He's so precious. . . ."

Brennan stroked the baby's cheek. "I would give the world for you to open your eyes, son. My little boy, do you have any idea how much you are loved?" His voice broke. "Your mother and I love you so much."

Leaning forward, he kissed the baby. In the next instant, Brennan was gone.

Amanda placed a hand on Elle's shoulder. "Your son is in heaven, baby."

"I know, Mama. I know I'm being selfish, but I want my baby with me." Her tears came harder. There was nothing anybody could say or do to diminish the loss she felt. She grieved for the child who'd never had a chance to live.

Elle went upstairs to rest after the funeral services for Brennan Edward Cunningham IV. For the first time ever, she didn't relish being around friends and family.

Since coming home from the hospital, Elle hadn't done much but sleep. She hardly left the room and barely ate. There were no words for what she felt. Elle was bewildered by the sadness that overwhelmed her.

Brennan came up to check on her. "How are you feeling?"

"As well as can be expected, I guess."

"Jillian's fixing a plate for you. Melina will bring it up."

Elle nodded, but she wasn't hungry. Turning to her side, she closed her eyes. She was very aware that she was shutting Brennan out, but there was nothing she could do about it. Her only child was dead. Her husband's grief was not as deep as hers, because he still had a child.

Through her grief, resentment grew. Charis was a mean-spirited woman, and she had Lauren. Brennan had married Elle only because she'd been carrying his child. Now that their son was gone, where did that leave them?

If her husband decided to leave her, Elle couldn't blame him. She had failed him.

* * *

Brennan watched her a moment, then left the room. His mother met him on the stairs.

"How is she?"

"I don't know. I don't think I've ever seen her so sad."

"I suppose that's understandable."

"She's sleeping now. You can see her later."

Elizabeth nodded. "I'm sorry for your loss," she said in a low voice.

"Thank you, Mother."

Brennan sighed in frustration before walking back into the formal living room, where everyone had gathered. He held back his desire for everybody to leave. Like Elle, he wasn't up for company. He and his wife needed time alone to grieve, something they hadn't been allowed to do since their son's death.

Carrie handed Brennan a plate laden with food. "You should eat something," she advised.

He thanked her as he accepted the plate.

She looked like she wanted to say more, but she must have changed her mind, because she moved on. Brennan was grateful. He didn't want to talk to anyone.

Two hours later, everyone had gone home. Melina came down the stairs carrying the tray of untouched food from their bedroom. Elle was still not eating, and it worried him.

Brennan strolled out on the terrace. Watching the sunset, he felt his armor slip. All that had happened rushed to the forefront, and he could not contain the pain. Sobbing, he fell back into one of the chairs.

* * *

Elle eased out of bed, acutely aware of the soreness she still felt. It was a week ago today that this nightmare had begun. Pressing her hand to her stomach, she made her way to the door.

Melina met her at the bottom of the stairs. "Can I get you something, Mrs. Cunningham?"

She shook her head. "No, I'm fine. Please call me Elle. I insist." Glancing around, she asked, "Did everyone leave?"

"Yes."

"Brennan, too?"

Melina pointed toward the terrace. "He's out there."

"Thank you," Elle murmured. She headed in that direction. She could hear his crying, and it tore at her insides. This was her fault. If she'd listened to him and slowed down, maybe none of this would have happened. How would she ever make this up to him?

The next morning, Brennan was able to coax Elle into having breakfast with him. She only ate a spoonful of fruit and a piece of toast, but it was a start.

After breakfast, Elle went back up to their room.

Three hours later, Brennan went in search of her. "I thought we could take a walk. You haven't been to see the rose garden lately."

"Maybe another time."

To him she still looked tired and pale, with a brightness in her eyes that was not natural. "Honey, you need some fresh air. We'll take a short walk; then you can come back here and rest."

"I don't feel like it, Brennan."

"I'm not going to take no for an answer. I'm not going to sit here and let you become a hermit." He strolled over to the walk-in closet and pulled out a dress. "Here. Put this on."

Elle waited several beats before she did as she was told.

Brennan tried to get her to open up during their stroll, but she wasn't in a talkative mood. Finally he gave up and settled for her silence.

When they returned to the house, Elle surprised him by curling up on the couch in the media room. Brennan dropped down beside her.

"Interested in watching a movie?" he asked.

"Not really. You can watch whatever you'd like." Picking up a book, she said, "I'll finish reading this."

In the middle of the movie Brennan was watching, the phone rang.

He answered it on the second ring. It was Charis.

"I was so sorry to hear about your loss."

"Thank you." He stole a peek at Elle.

"You sound so terribly sad," Charis interjected. "I think I know what will lift your spirits."

"What's that?"

"A visit with Lauren. It would be good for you."

Brennan glanced over at Elle a second time. She appeared to be engrossed in whatever she was reading.

"Did you hear what I said?" Charis asked.

"Yes, I heard you." He considered what she said for a moment. "I'll be there in about an hour."

"Wonderful. We'll see you then."

When he hung up, Elle asked, "Who was that?"

"Charis." He felt guilty, but didn't understand why. Lauren was his daughter.

"You're going to her house?"

"I thought I would go get Lauren and take her to the park." Brennan tried to gauge her reaction. "Would you like to come along?"

Elle shook her head furiously.

"Would you rather I stay home with you?"

"No. Go spend time with your . . . your daughter."

She'd practically spat the words out. Brennan stared at her for a moment before rising to his feet. "Are you sure you're okay with this?"

"I said go." That time she'd almost bitten his head off. Brennan yearned to help Elle, but he didn't know how. She was in so much pain, but she kept shutting him out. It was as if she were the only one grieving. She wasn't. Brennan grieved for his son, too.

He left the house, feeling more and more like a heel the closer he got to his car. Brennan glanced back at the house. It had never seemed so lonely as it did lately.

Elle hated herself at the moment. She was angry. Angry that her baby hadn't survived; angry that Brennan was leaving to spend time with his daughter and Charis. Memories of her son and what might have been stirred her grief to the surface.

At the moment life seemed so unfair.

The phone rang, scaring Elle. She answered it. "Hello."

"Hey, sis. It's Kaitlin. I thought you might want to take a ride with me to Laine's."

"No, thanks. I don't want to go over there."

"Why not?"

"I don't want to see Regis."

Kaitlin was silent for a moment.

Elle sighed loudly. "I know how mean that sounds," she admitted, "but it's the way I feel."

"No, I understand. Really, I do. You just lost your son. I felt the same way when I lost little Matthew. Only I was alone in Mexico. I didn't have my family or Matt to help me through my grief."

"I know you guys are there for me, but I'm tired of people asking what could it have been. Or they ask if I had a feeling something was wrong. I didn't notice anything. I just thought the baby was quiet. I didn't know anything was wrong." Elle's voice was filled with tears. "I didn't know, and I feel so bad."

"Honey, guilt is a piece of grief. It's a part of trying to make sense of all that's happened. You did nothing wrong."

"I don't know, Kaitlin. I think Brennan may blame me for this. He kept after me to stop traveling and working such long hours."

"Elle, it's going to take some time to resolve your feelings. I promise you that it does get a little easier over time. There are times I still cry over Matthew."

"It's so unfair."

"I know, sis. When you're ready, you and Brennan will try again."

"I don't know about that. I'm afraid something will go wrong again. Besides, I don't even know if I'll have a husband by then."

"I have no intentions of going anywhere, Elle. I will be your husband until you decide you don't want me to be," Brennan announced from across the room.

"I think I'll let you go," Kaitlin stated. "You and your hubby need to talk."

Elle hung up. Nervous, she chewed on her bottom lip.

"I decided I couldn't leave you like this. We've suffered a devastating loss, and we have to find a way to get through our grief *together*." Brennan pulled her up gently. Embracing her, he said, "We will get through this."

Elle held on to him as tightly as she could. "I . . . I thought I was doing everything right." Her voice broke. She stood slumped, all of her energy spent.

"Honey, the doctor said there was nothing we could have done to prevent this from happening. . . ." Brennan kissed her cheek. "It wasn't your fault."

They stood there in front of the marble fireplace holding each other, their tears mingling, uniting their grief.

Chapter Eleven

Elle's mind was congested with doubts and fears. Shortly, they would be heading to her in-laws. This would be her first time seeing them since the funeral.

Brennan slipped on a pullover shirt. He glanced at her while tucking it into his pants. "Why do you look as if you've lost your best friend?"

"I'm not so sure about this. Your parents aren't pleased with our marriage, so why are they having this brunch?" Was this another attempt to humiliate her? She couldn't help but wonder.

Brennan embraced her. "Nothing is going to happen to you, sweetheart. I won't let Mother insult you. My father never has much to say, so you don't have to worry about him."

"Well, I'm glad my family will be there, too. I think I'll feel more comfortable."

"Besides, Pookie is the one hosting this brunch. It's not my mother. She wanted to have a reception in our honor, but after everything that happened, she thought this would be more appropriate."

"Oh, that's right. She did mention that. With her vacation in Africa, your traveling, and then my having to travel, our schedules didn't mesh. I'd forgotten all about the reception."

"We should leave now so we won't be late."

Elle followed Brennan out to the car. She silently prayed that all would go well today. Since the baby's death, she hadn't felt much like socializing, but Brennan had convinced her to leave the confines of their estate. It was time to move on, he'd said.

When they arrived twenty minutes later, the first person Elle saw was Charis Wentworth. She sighed in irritation.

Pookie was quick to explain. "I didn't invite her. I don't mind marching over there and telling her to leave."

"It's okay. I'm not going to let her get to me. Especially not today."

"Good girl . . ."

Randall eased up behind them. "Hello, Aunt Pookie. Elle, welcome to the family. I'm sorry about your loss."

She embraced him. "Thank you, Randall. It's good to see you again."

"If you need anything, just let me know, okay?"

Elle nodded.

He looked as if he were about to say something else when Charis swooped over and took Randall by the arm, interrupting their conversation. "Hello, darling. I've been looking for you. My mother's been dying to see you since you've been back in town."

They quickly moved on, but not before Elle glimpsed the angry looks exchanged between Charis and Randall.

She was almost positive that there was something going on between them. *But what?*

She stopped one of the waiters and requested a glass of water. Scanning the room, Elle searched for a familiar face. Her family should have arrived by now. She soon spotted her mother and Regis. Her eyes strayed briefly to Regis's protruding stomach. A wave of pain washed over her.

Before Elle could join them, she was stopped by Muffin, who embraced her. "How are you, dear?"

"I'm fine, Miss Worthington. It's so good to see you again. How are the wedding plans coming along?"

"You know, I've tried to convince Steven to elope, but he's always so busy. At this rate, someone will have to wheel me down the aisle." She broke into a tiny laugh. "Actually, Steven and I are planning to have a small ceremony on the first Saturday in June."

"That's wonderful," Elle exclaimed.

"What's so wonderful?" Brennan asked as he joined them.

"Muffin's going to marry your uncle in a couple of months."

"It's about time." He reached over, hugging her tightly. "Congratulations."

"Excuse me, please. I need to go to the bathroom," Elle announced. "I'll be back shortly."

In the bathroom, she relieved herself and touched up her makeup. When she came out, Elle found herself face-to-face with Elizabeth. "Mrs. Cunningham, what can I do for you?"

"I just wanted to formally welcome you into the Cunningham family. With everything that happened ... well, my son obviously *believes* you are the woman for him."

Elle didn't miss the woman's intended barb.

"I trust you will make him very happy."

"I intend to do my best, Mrs. Cunningham. I love him very much."

"I'm sure you mean it." She gave a small sigh. "It's a shame, however, that his daughter will have to grow up without her father."

"I'm sure Brennan will spend as much time with her as he can. I do not intend to keep him from her."

"I have to be honest. It just seems to me that he would rethink this marriage. His daughter is here and . . . well . . ."

"What are you saying?" Elle was angry now. "How dare you!"

Pookie interrupted them. "Lizbeth, what are you saying? The poor girl has been through enough." She placed a protective arm around Elle.

"I was merely pointing out that Brennan's daughter should be given a chance to grow up with her father."

"How do you know that the child is really Brennan's?" Pookie challenged. "Charis is not the most honest person around. The woman is a slut."

Elizabeth gasped.

"Well, she is," Pookie said calmly.

Elle chose this moment to walk away. She'd had enough of Brennan's mother.

"We have not finished our conversation—" Elizabeth began.

"Yes, we have," Elle threw back. "I don't want to disrespect you, Mrs. Cunningham, so I'm ending this conversation right now."

"There is no need for theatrics, *Miss Ransom*. I was only voicing my opinion."

"Apparently it wasn't welcomed," Pookie stated. "So

why don't you find someone else who might actually be interested in hearing whatever it is you have to say?''

Elizabeth rolled her eyes heavenward. "I wish you'd mind your business for a change and stay out of mine.''

"Fine," Pookie said testily. "At the rate you're going, you will soon find yourself all alone. Don't say I didn't warn you.''

Elle didn't know whether to cry or just be outraged. She and her mother-in-law would never be close. They would merely tolerate each other, and that fact made her sad.

"Honey, what's wrong?" Amanda asked. "You look like you're about to cry.''

Elle tearfully repeated Elizabeth's words.

"What a horrible thing to say to you," Amanda sputtered, bristling with indignation. "I should go over there and straighten out that terrible woman.''

"It's okay, Mama. I think I made my point." Elle tried to stop her mother, but it was already too late. As soon as Amanda caught sight of Elizabeth, she crossed the room in determined strides with the aid of her quad cane.

"Mrs. Cunningham, I want to have a word with you.'' Amanda's voice was cold and lashing.

Elizabeth's eyes briefly met Elle's before she nodded.

A swift shadow of anger swept across Amanda's face. "This is a somewhat strange situation we have all found ourselves in, but the truth of the matter is that your son and my daughter are married. I must admit that I'm not totally in agreement with this marriage.''

"I'm sure your daughter gave you her version—''

"She merely repeated what you said to her.''

Elizabeth's eyes shifted to Elle once more. "Your daughter misunderstood me. I am saddened by the loss of her child."

Amanda's fawn-colored eyes darkened like angry thunderclouds. "You mean your grandchild, don't you?"

"I know that."

"Then you also need to know that my daughter loves Brennan. She has loved him for a long time."

"Why are you telling me this?" Elizabeth's voice was quiet, yet held an undertone of cold contempt.

"You're so worried about your precious bloodline and whether or not a Ransom is suited to a Cunningham. Well, I have the same issues, because I'm not sure your son deserves Elle. I'm not sure you or your rich blood deserve to even breathe the very air that she does. Frankly, my baby girl is much too good for you and your family."

Elizabeth's mouth dropped open in shock.

"How dare you look down your nose at my daughter!" Amanda's voice rose an octave. "Wealth does not equal happiness, and it certainly does not equal love. You think we're so beneath you, but I have news for you. For all of your fine clothes, fine home and furnishings, your big bank accounts . . ." Amanda's voice died as she shook her head sadly. "I feel so sorry for you. You have no idea what it's like to have compassion for another person—"

"How dare you!" Elizabeth cut in rudely. "You don't know what you're talking about."

"You are a cold woman, Mrs. Cunningham. Your heart is cold, and I feel sorry for you." Turning her back on Elizabeth, Amanda took Elle's hand. "Honey, I'm afraid I'm going to have to leave. I just can't stand another minute in this beautifully decorated mauso-leum." With Elle's help, she headed to the door.

"Amanda," Elizabeth called out.

Turning around, Amanda stated, "*It's Mrs. Ransom to you.* Furthermore, we have nothing else to say to each other."

"Mama, I wish you would reconsider," Elle pleaded. "Please don't leave."

Amanda shook her head. "No, baby. This is not for me."

"I'll go with you. We can all go back to Jillian's house or Laine's and have a cookout or something."

"Honey, you need to stay here with your husband. You have to consider his feelings now. Not just your own."

Laine spoke up. "Regis and I aren't leaving. We're going to be here with you." He placed a comforting hand on Elle's shoulder. "I think Kaitlin and Matt are staying around, too."

She turned to Nyle. "Are you and Chandra leaving?"

He shook his head. "We'll be here for another hour or so."

"I'm sorry about this."

"It's not your fault, Elle. Brennan's mother is an iceberg. You had nothing to do with that." Kaitlin embraced her sister. "She's lucky Mama got to her before I did."

Her comment brought a smile to Elle's face. "I'm glad you're in my corner."

"Here comes your hubby," Laine announced dryly.

Elle met him halfway. "I guess you heard," Elle mut-tered. "I'm so sorry things got nasty."

"Don't be," Brennan reassured her with a tender smile. "I'm sure Mother had it coming."

For the rest of the evening, Elle decided to avoid Elizabeth. Needing a breath of fresh air, she took a stroll outside. She needed a minute to clear her head.

Regis came out to join her after a while.

"Elle, can we talk for a minute?"

"Sure." She kept her gaze straight ahead.

"I'm so sorry." Regis paused. "I feel a little guilty, too."

Elle turned to her in surprise. "Why?"

"Because I know how much it hurts you to see me like this."

"I love you, Regis. I really do. I guess I know how Laine used to feel when he thought he couldn't father a child. On one hand I'm thrilled that you and Laine are having another baby, but on the other, I resent it. It's my problem and I'm dealing with it. Just know that I love you and I'm trying."

Regis nodded. "I love you, too." She gestured to the door. "Laine's probably looking for me."

"You go on. I need a few more minutes."

"Okay." Regis headed back inside.

Tossing a look over her shoulder, Elle said, "Regis, take care of yourself. I want a healthy niece."

Smiling, Regis nodded.

When she felt stronger, Elle came back inside.

Charis cornered her in the hallway. "Oh, there you are. I suppose you're feeling very pleased with yourself," she accused.

"What are you talking about?"

"Convincing Brennan to run off with you like that. Then keeping him away from us for almost a month."

"It was Brennan's idea to elope. So was the honey-moon."

"It won't change anything." Charis spat out the words contemptuously. "The only thing your marriage has done is declare war between us. You see, I'm not going to let you keep Lauren from her father."

"I have no intentions of keeping Lauren from anything," Elle retorted. She permitted herself a withering stare. "However, I *do* intend to keep you away from my husband."

Charis shot Elle a cold look. "I guess we'll just have to see how long he'll remain your husband. Brennan and I belong together. Even his parents realize that. Your elopement has only delayed the inevitable a little. In the end, Brennan will pay you a tidy settlement to disappear."

Elle's breath came raggedly in impotent anger. "You seem to conveniently dismiss the fact that he still married me after finding out about Lauren. Say what you'd like, but I'm giving you fair warning. Brennan is now my husband, and I'm not going to stand back and let you take him. If you want a fight—so be it. Now move out of my way."

"I—"

Elle cut her off by saying, "Save it for someone who cares." As soon as she found Brennan, she stated, "I've had enough of your family and Charis. I'm ready to go home." She held her breath as she waited for the argument that was sure to come.

It didn't. Brennan simply nodded and said his good-byes.

* * *

The following weekend, Brennan wished for a way to get out of spending an evening with the Ransoms. Tonight he just wanted a quiet evening at home with his wife. But Elle was looking forward to seeing her family. They were all having dinner at La Maison to celebrate Regis and Laine's wedding anniversary.

From behind him, Elle said, "You look very handsome."

He turned around. "Thank you, sweetheart." Brennan's eyes traveled over her body. "You look as beautiful as ever."

An hour later, they headed to La Maison. Most of her family had already arrived by the time they got there. Elle greeted everyone while Brennan hung back. Several minutes passed before she even realized he wasn't standing beside her.

Elle seemed more like herself around her family. Even some of the color had returned in her face. He was relieved to see she was slowly returning to normal.

Jillian ambled over to him. "Hello, Brennan. I'm glad you could make it."

Staring at her gravely, he finally said, "I wouldn't miss it."

"I've never been one to beat around the bush. My sister is a very sweet and loving person. Don't you dare take that from her. Losing her child . . ." Jillian paused. "It was extremely hard on Elle."

"When *our* son died, I suffered just as greatly. Jillian, I have no intentions of hurting my wife."

Her steady gaze met his. "See that you don't. Because if you do—you'll have to answer to me."

A slight smile on his face, Brennan said, "I will consider myself warned." Stepping around her, he said, "Now, if you will excuse me, I intend to join my wife."

As he moved around the room, Brennan caught a few of Elle's family members studying him from head to toe. He read in their faces the same assessment he held for them. They would not be close or even friends—they would simply tolerate each other.

"So, did you have a good time tonight?" Brennan asked Elle when they returned home.

"I did." She slipped off her dress and placed it on a padded hanger. Looking over her shoulder, she asked, "What about you? You looked like you were bored out of your mind."

"I'm not much into family." Seeing her undressed and standing in a lacy bra and matching panties, Brennan reached for her. "Come here."

Elle tensed. She recognized the look of lust in his eyes. Her doctor had already given the okay for them to resume their physical relationship, but she wasn't ready for sex.

"I miss you, sweetheart." Brennan tried to kiss her.

She retreated a step, holding up her hands to keep him away. "Please don't . . ."

He drew back, asking, "What's wrong?"

"Nothing. I just want to take a shower." Elle walked briskly, wanting to escape the huskiness of his voice, the air of blatant sexuality that surrounded him—she wanted to get away from her husband.

Brennan was standing in the bathroom when she stepped out of the shower. His eyes grazed over her. Elle could feel them on her damp hair and all over her naked body. His glance did not rest on any particular feature longer than any other. He gave equal attention to the water droplets on her shoulders, in the hollow of her throat, outlining her breasts and running down to her stomach.

Feeling self-conscious, she asked, "Why are you just staring at me like that?"

"I've never seen you look more beautiful." Pulling her into his arms, Brennan kissed her. "I don't want you catching a cold." He released her and reached for a nearby bath towel.

Elle stood as still as a statue while Brennan dried her off. She put on the black silk nightgown he held out to her.

"Ready to tell me what's going on with you?"

She shivered. Folding her arms across her chest, Elle whispered, "Nothing. I don't know."

"I want to make love to you."

A flicker of anxiety coursed through her. "I can't, Brennan. I'm just not ready."

A chill black silence enveloped the room.

"It's time we get our lives back to normal, sweetheart," Brennan stated gently. Touching her face lightly, he added, "The doctor said we could try again in a few months."

The color drained from Elle's face. "Having another baby won't make me forget my son."

"I know that," Brennan snapped. He lowered his voice. "I'm sorry. I didn't mean to snap."

Feeling like her composure was under attack, she turned away from him, saying, "I'm tired. I just want to go to bed and get some sleep. If we continue this discussion, we're going to end up fighting."

"Maybe you're right. Let's just go to bed."

That night sleep didn't come easy for Elle. Her eyes wouldn't close and her mind wouldn't rest. Lying there beside her husband, she had never felt more alone in her life.

Chapter Twelve

Brennan was distant the next morning. When Elle's attempts to engage him in conversation were unsuccessful, she gave up and retreated to her office.

He came to see her an hour later. "I'm leaving for D.C. later tonight. I'll be gone for a week."

Elle stared at him in surprise. "When did you decide this?"

"I just got off the phone with my father. He wants me to take in a couple of meetings for him. Mother has been pestering him to take her to London."

She felt ice spreading through her stomach. "Oh." Elle tried to hide her inner misery from his probing stare.

"You can come with me if you'd like," Brennan suggested.

"Are you sure?"

He nodded.

Elle thought about it. Maybe it would do them both some good to get away. "I'll go upstairs and pack."

Upstairs, Elle searched through the massive walk-in closet for clothes to take with her on her trip. She chose several dresses and a couple of pairs of pants with matching tops. To wear on the plane, she selected a linen shirt and matching lavender drawstring pants.

With grim determination, she didn't look at the section of brand-new maternity clothes hanging near the back of the closet. Brennan had made Melina move them there. Elle shook her head, trying to force away the pain. While she dressed, she fought to keep her tears at bay. Finally, she covered her face with trembling hands and gave vent to the agony of her loss.

While Brennan endured two days of meetings and seminars, Elle took a tour of Washington, D.C. Although she'd been there on several occasions, she always enjoyed playing tourist and shopping. At the end of the day, she was driven back to the Willard Inter-Continental Hotel, where they were staying.

Elle adored the hotel where Julia Ward Howe had composed the Civil War anthem, "The Battle Hymn of the Republic," in 1861. They were staying in what was known as the Jenny Lind Suite, which was furnished to resemble a French garret and offered a grand view of the Washington Monument.

Brennan arrived shortly after her. Elle poured him a glass of wine and handed it to him.

"Thanks, sweetheart. What did you do today?"

"I went to see the White House and other prominent D.C. tourist attractions." Elle settled back on the couch and crossed her legs. "How was your day?"

"Do you realize we haven't had any real conversation

since we've been here?" Brennan's response held a note of impatience.

Elle frowned in annoyance. "Don't start. I am doing the best I can."

"We're meeting my cousin Jensen for dinner."

She searched her memory. "Jensen? Is he one of Jordan's brothers?"

"Yes." He took off his jacket and headed to the shower.

"What's he doing here?" Elle asked when he came out fifteen minutes later. "I thought he lived in North Carolina somewhere."

"He lives in Raleigh. My father summoned him to D.C. to help me. Apparently he didn't think I could handle the training platforms alone."

"Brennan, I'm sorry."

He waved off her apology. "We have eight o'clock reservations," he said tersely. "You should change."

"I'll be ready." Elle made her way to the bathroom. True to her word, she was ready by the time they had to leave.

They met Jensen at the Willard Room, one of Washington's most elegant restaurants, housed inside their hotel.

Brennan quickly made the introductions before they were seated.

He lapsed into a discussion about business with Jensen while Elle scanned the dinner menu. A few minutes later, he asked, "Have you decided on what you want to eat?"

Elle nodded. "I'm going to have the shrimp pasta."

"That sounds good," Jensen stated. "I think I'll have that, too."

She smiled at Brennan. "What are you going to have?"

He scanned the menu once more. "I think I'll have the shrimp pasta as well."

Elle could tell Brennan was still upset with her. He would barely glance her way. She couldn't wait for this night to finally come to an end.

The waiter took their orders and returned fifteen minutes later with their meals.

The discussion over dinner turned to books, since they were all avid readers. By the time dessert arrived, they were all laughing and having a good time.

Back inside their suite, Brennan was once again in a solemn mood.

As they readied for bed, Elle said, "I'm beginning to think I made a mistake coming here."

He surprised her by saying, "I agree."

"What?"

"It's obvious even to me that you would prefer to continue grieving than trying to pick up the pieces of our life together. We barely talk anymore unless there's someone else around. And as for sex—that's totally out of the question."

"I'm sorry I'm not like you, Brennan. I can't just stop my heart from breaking into pieces over my son."

"He was my son, too!" he yelled.

Startled by his unexpected outburst, Elle jumped. Wiping away her tears, she tried to speak but couldn't.

Picking up the phone, he said, "I'll arrange for you to fly back to Los Angeles tomorrow morning."

It was already starting, Elle thought miserably. Their marriage was a farce and would soon come to an end. Perhaps Brennan wouldn't leave her, but Elle wasn't sure she was strong enough to withstand the strain.

She could fight for him, her heart advised. Elle glanced over to where Brennan stood. Her breath caught at the sight. She loved him still.

That night she prayed in earnest. Elle needed divine guidance and she needed strength. She was going to try and save her marriage.

Melina greeted Elle upon her return. She took the garment bag from Elle, saying, "Mr. Cunningham called to see if you'd made it home safe. He said he tried your cell phone but you didn't answer."

"I didn't hear it ringing." Elle stood at the bottom of the stairs. "I'm going to take a nap. I couldn't sleep on the plane."

"I'll wake you when dinner is ready."

"Thank you, Melina." Elle made her way up the stairs and to her room.

By the time she'd changed and made herself comfortable, Melina arrived with a tray.

"I didn't think you'd want to eat at that great big table by yourself."

Elle forced a smile.

"Robert and I are going to retire early, if you don't need us."

"That's fine with me. I'm not going to be up too late myself. I was going to do some work, but I've changed my mind. I'm just going to relax with a good book."

"I'll be back for the tray—"

Elle cut her off by saying, "No, don't bother. I'll take it down to the kitchen myself. Just enjoy your evening with your husband, Melina."

"It's no bother."

"I insist. I will take it down."

"Mrs. Cunningham, my boss is a very lucky man."

Elle hugged her. "Thank you, Melina. I'm very blessed to have Brennan in my life. He's a wonderful man, and I feel bad. I haven't been the wife I should be."

"You lost your baby. Mr. Cunningham has suffered, too. He understands. During this time you two need each other."

"You're right, Melina."

For a moment Elle looked serious, almost sad. "I'll see you in the morning."

Melina smiled as she made her way to the door. "Rest well, Mrs. Cunningham."

"I really wish you'd call me Elle."

Making herself comfortable on the couch, she dug into the chicken fingers and french fries. As she ate, her heart pounded with unexpected intensity. Would she ever feel normal again? Elle wondered. If she didn't do something soon, their marriage was not going to be an amicable one.

When she finished eating, Elle decided to indulge herself in a hot bubble bath. She lay back in the tub, letting the hot, soapy water soothe away the tension in her body.

Soon after she dragged herself out of the Jacuzzi, the phone rang. Elle rushed to answer it.

"Hello."

"How are you?"

Elle smiled. "I'm fine, Brennan. How are things going?"

"Great. I might be able to come home tomorrow."

Pulling the towel closer around her, Elle trembled. "Really?"

"Yes. I hope that we'll be able to sit down and talk. I mean really talk. I can't go on the way things are."

Elle didn't say a word. Truth was, she didn't know what to say.

"Are you still there?" Brennan asked.

"I'm here. Will you call me tomorrow and let me know if you're coming home for sure?"

"Sure, if that's what you want."

They talked for a few more minutes before hanging up.

Elle slipped on an oversize T-shirt and a pair of leggings. She sat in the middle of her bed, hugging her knees. Brennan might be coming home as early as tomorrow. She wasn't quite ready to see him yet. So what was she going to do?

Brennan dropped his suitcase in the foyer. When Melina bent to pick it up, he said, "Leave it, please. I'll take it upstairs later."

"I had Robert prepare a steak and salad for you. It should be ready shortly."

Raising his eyebrow, he asked, "How did you know I would be arriving today?"

"Mrs. Cunningham told me."

Brennan had spoken to Elle that morning. "I see. Where is my wife?"

Melina frowned. "I assumed she'd already told you. Mrs. Cunningham left a few hours ago for Las Vegas. She's going to be there for a few days."

Brennan searched his memory. Elle hadn't mentioned anything about a trip to Vegas. Pulling out his cell phone, he called Malcolm.

After a few words, Brennan asked, "Is Elle there on business?"

"She's there with Treach. I expect she'll be back in a day or so." Malcolm's laughter traveled through the phone. "Missing your wife?"

"Not for long. I'm going to surprise her in Las Vegas. Don't you breathe a word to Elle, Malcolm. It's a surprise."

"I won't. I think it's a good idea. Elle hasn't seemed like herself in a while. With everything you've both had to endure—I understand why."

"It's been real hard on us both," Brennan acknowledged. "But Elle's taken the worse of it. I miss her a lot."

When Brennan hung up on Malcolm, he called and made arrangements to have his plane fueled and ready.

He was not going to let Elle wither away in her grief.

Elle closed her eyes and, for just a moment, she was aware only of the yearning Brennan aroused in her. She'd been having a bad day until she heard his voice on the telephone.

"You're a hard lady to keep up with," he teased.

"I left the hotel information with Melina, so it couldn't have been that difficult."

"So, what are you going to do tonight?"

"Let's see. I'm going to order room service and watch TV. Why?"

"I don't know. I thought maybe you and Treach might decide to do a little sight-seeing, maybe gamble or take in one of the shows."

"I don't have a clue what Treach plans to do. Besides, he and I don't travel in the same circles." Switching the phone to her other ear, Elle asked, "Why are you so concerned with what I'm going to do tonight? It's not like you're here with me."

"What would you do if I were?"

"Hmmmmm . . . I don't know. I guess we would order something to eat and just curl up together and talk."

Brennan chuckled. "Really?"

"Yes." Smiling, Elle asked, "Do you have a different scenario?"

"Maybe." His tone was noncommittal. "I think it would start with me bringing you two dozen roses; then the waiter would arrive with champagne and dinner. After dessert, we would play some soft romantic music and dance. Looking into each other's eyes, we would hold each other and . . ." He stopped short.

"And what?" Elle questioned.

"I'll leave it to your imagination."

There was a knock on her door.

"Who is that?" Brennan asked.

Puzzled, Elle answered, "I don't know. I haven't ordered my food yet." She rose and strolled over to the door.

"Sweetheart?" Brennan prompted.

"I'm still here." Elle glanced through the peephole. Her breath caught and she blinked twice. She couldn't believe Brennan was there in Vegas. Throwing open the door, she asked, "What are you doing here?"

Removing the cell phone from his ear, he replied, "I came to collect my wife." He held out a bouquet of roses in an assortment of vivid colors. "These are for you."

She was silent for a moment, fighting her emotions. "Thank you, Brennan." Biting her lip, Elle looked away.

"You're also running away. I just need to know why."

"I wanted some time alone," she muttered uneasily. "I needed time to think." She walked across the room to return the cordless phone to its cradle.

"About what?" Brennan wanted to know.

Holding the roses close to her, Elle answered, "About us. You married me because I was carrying your child. That was the glue holding us together."

Brennan hesitated, measuring her for a moment. "You can't really believe that."

Giving him a narrowed, glinting glance, she asked, "Are you saying there's more?" Elle carried the bouquet over to the wet bar, where she filled a pitcher with water and stuck the flowers in it.

Brennan followed her. "I think so," Brennan confessed. "I care for you. I want our marriage to work, Elle." He turned her around so that she was facing him. "I need you in my life."

She searched anxiously for the meaning behind his words. "But is that enough to hold our marriage together? You have Lauren. Brennan, she deserves a full-time father. You can be that for her—just divorce me."

His expression was that of someone who had been struck in the face. "Divorce is out of the question. I want to have another child, sweetheart. *With you.* I want us to be a family."

"I'm scared, Brennan."

He pulled her into his arms. "Of what?"

"What if I'm one of those women who can't carry a child—"

"Get rid of those thoughts," Brennan cut in. "You mustn't think this way. The doctor said . . ." He stopped. "I don't mean to push you. I really don't."

"It really means a lot to you to have another child, doesn't it? I just don't want to disappoint you."

"You could never do that," he reassured her.

"Could you please give me some time, Brennan?"

"I will try, sweetheart. I desperately want to make love to you, but I will wait until you're ready."

"Thank you." Hugging him back, she said, "I really needed to hear you say that." Elle laid her head on his chest. "I missed you, too."

When she heard the soft knock on the door, Elle lifted her head. "Now, who could that be?"

"Probably room service," Brennan announced. "I ordered dinner for us."

He opened the door and took care of the waiter. Elle stood back, smiling.

While they ate, Brennan and Elle talked. It was the first real conversation they'd had in a while. True to his word, they danced after dessert to a special CD of songs he'd recorded just for her.

In bed that night, Elle and Brennan held each other until they fell asleep. The closeness she'd once felt with Brennan was back.

Chapter Thirteen

A breeze fluttered through the curtain at the bedroom window, bringing in a welcome draft of spring air. Today would be perfect, if only Elle could get out of today's plans.

Brennan was downstairs in the media room when she came down. He glanced over his shoulder at her. "Ready?"

She nodded. "As ready as I can be."

"Why do you sound like you're on your way to prison or something?"

Elle chewed on her bottom lip. "I really don't feel like dealing with your mother and Charis today. Besides, you're planning to spend time with Lauren, so I don't really need to be here. I could drive out to my mother's house and see my family."

Brennan glanced over at her. "I want you here. Pookie's coming with Muffin, so the three of you can catch up."

Gathering her courage and smoothing back her curly

hair into a semblance of neatness, Elle decided to be honest about her feelings. "I'm still very angry with your mother."

"I understand that, Elle, and she deserves it, but I think she wants to make amends."

Sighing in resignation, Elle shrugged. "Whatever."

An uneasy silence settled between them.

"Sweetheart, I realize you're in a lot of pain. So am I, but we have to find a way to go on." Brennan studied his wife for a moment. "We can't just stop living. You can't avoid babies or pregnant women. I've noticed the way you look at your sister-in-law."

Elle's eyes watered. "It's just not that easy, Brennan. I miss my baby so much. My arms ache from wanting to hold him."

He hugged her. "So do I, honey. I miss him, too."

She could see the pain etched on her husband's face.

Clearing his throat, Brennan released her. "Our guests should be arriving soon."

"I'm going to check with Robert on the food." Elle headed to the kitchen. She really hated the idea of being home today. Being around Charis and her mother-in-law was more than she wanted to deal with at the moment.

Everyone would be at her mother's house today. Even though it was becoming increasingly harder for her to be around Regis in her advanced state of pregnancy, she wanted to spend some time with her own family. She shook off her disappointment.

Satisfied that everything was perfect in the kitchen, Elle returned to the front of the house, joining Brennan in the formal living room.

Charis rang the doorbell a few minutes later.

Opening the door, Elle locked eyes with her.

Awarding Elle with a hostile glare, she said snidely, "I didn't know you were going to be here."

"Hello to you, too," Elle replied dryly as Brennan joined her.

Brushing past her, Charis spoke to Brennan. "I'm so glad you want to spend time with your daughter. Lauren needs her father."

Looking outside, Elle inquired, "Where is Lauren?"

"The governess is getting her out of the car. They should be in in a moment."

Charis's governess, Ariel, walked in carrying the toddler. Practically snatching the child from the woman, Charis cooed, "Come on, sweetie. Time to say hello to Daddy."

She sounds so fake, Elle thought to herself. *Charis probably doesn't spend any time with the little girl.* Elle kept her anger in check. It was so unfair that her child had been taken away from her.

She could tell that Brennan was getting upset. "I'm not going to let her disrespect you any longer," he whispered when she joined him.

Charis had already seated herself on the sofa and was playing with Lauren. Elle gestured for Ariel to take a seat.

Elle laid a hand on Brennan's arm. "It's okay, honey. She's only trying to push my buttons, and I'm not going to give her that kind of power over me. Just enjoy your daughter." She took Brennan's hand.

Catching sight of their expression of unity, Charis glowered. Holding out the toddler, she said, "Take your daughter, please. She's getting so heavy."

Elle knew exactly what Charis was doing. She also didn't miss the triumphant look on her face when Brennan picked up his daughter. Disgusted, she turned away.

They had moved into the family room when the door-bell sounded again. Elle stood up to answer it, but Brennan stilled her.

"Let Melina get it. It's her job."

She soon heard Pookie's cheerful voice and smiled in relief. When Elle saw Muffin, she ran over and embraced her. "I'm so glad you and Pookie are here." Elle hugged Pookie next.

"We thought you might need some reinforcements," Muffin glanced over at Charis and whispered.

Stepping outside on the patio, Muffin and Pookie sat down at one of the round tables. Neither one of them wanted to be in the same room as Charis. Elle went out to talk to them.

"How are you feeling, sweetie?" Pookie asked.

"I wish I could say that each day it hurts less and less, but I can't. I would be lying."

Brennan eased up behind her, wrapping his arms around her. "We're taking one day at a time," he announced.

Elle turned around in his arms. Smiling, she stroked his cheek. "Thank God, we have each other," she murmured softly.

Coming out on the patio, Charis cleared her throat noisily. "Lauren's such a precious baby. Brennan and I are so fortunate to have her."

Muffin and Pookie exchanged looks.

"She's a beauty," Elle commented.

"What did you expect?" Charis sniped. "Look at her parents. We're not exactly hard on the eyes, you know."

"A simple thank-you would have been more than enough," Muffin murmured in a cultured voice. "One must always exercise good manners, Charis, dear."

Picking up Lauren, Charis rolled her eyes. "My

daughter is not on display for you people to gawk at," she snapped. "My goodness, you're scaring her."

Pookie broke into laughter. "Honey, with you as her mother, the child couldn't possibly scare that easily." She took a sip of her hot tea. "By the way, when was the child born?"

Charis seemed startled by Pookie's question. "Excuse me?"

"You heard me, Charis. I asked plain as day when the child was born. Speak up."

It was a moment before she answered. "Her birthday is in December."

Hiding her amusement, Elle joined Brennan in the kitchen. "Your aunts are giving Charis the third degree."

Brennan laughed. "They have never liked her."

Leaning against the counter, Elle smiled as the little girl peeked around the corner of the center island. When Elle waved, Lauren giggled and ran back out on the patio.

Through the doors, Elle heard Pookie utter, "Come here, Lauren. Let your Aunt Pookie take a look at you."

Charis wouldn't release her hold on the toddler.

"What's wrong?" Pookie asked in amusement. "Scared I might get a whiff of something?"

"I don't have anything to fear. The truth is on my side."

"Girl, who do you think you're talking to? I know you, Charis Wentworth. Don't you ever forget that."

"Miss Lake, I don't know why you don't like me. I've never done anything to you."

Pookie's response was nothing more than a snort. She waved her hand in dismissal. "Let me get out of here. . . ." She glanced over at Elle, who was coming in her direction. "Come take a walk through the rose gardens with me and Muffin. It's a beautiful day outside."

Brennan was falling in love. Elle watched Brennan with his daughter. It was obvious the little girl was stealing his heart.

Muffin gave her a sympathetic look. "Honey, are you okay with this?"

Elle could only nod. Her sense of loss was now beyond tears. "It hurts a little, but I can't keep Brennan from his daughter. It would be wrong." She sighed in resignation. "I just wish it would get easier."

Embracing her, Muffin assured her, "Everything will work itself out."

"I know."

"I must admit that I had my doubts at first, but the child does look like Brennan."

"Yes, she does," Elle agreed. "She looks every bit like her father."

"Well, I still don't believe it's as cut-and-dry as Charis says," Pookie announced. "That girl is hiding something. I can feel it in my bones."

Wrapping her arm around Pookie, Muffin said, "Give it up, dear. Brennan and Charis have a child. There's nothing any of us can do about it."

Elle caught sight of Brennan and Lauren running on the grounds. "He adores her," she murmured. She hadn't seen him this happy in a long time.

They were growing closer, and Elle realized just how much she'd missed him. Brennan had been right. It was time for them to try and rebuild the foundation that had been destroyed by the death of their son. She was finally ready.

Seeing Charis today had helped her come to this conclusion. Brennan was in a vulnerable state right now. If she wasn't careful, she could send him running back into Charis's waiting arms.

Brennan played with his daughter. Lauren was an adorable and very happy toddler.

"Are you having a good time, sweetie? Huh?" He tickled her under her chin and was awarded with a high-pitched giggle. Brennan reached out to pick up the toddler.

Grinning mischievously, Lauren quickly moved out of his grasp. He burst into laughter.

Brennan closed his eyes, pretending to fall asleep. He waited a few minutes, then grabbed the little girl. They both exploded into more laughter.

Lauren yawned sleepily and laid her head on his chest. Ariel made her way over to take the toddler, but Brennan shook his head.

"She's fine." He couldn't bear to let her go right this minute. Lauren had a grip on his heart and would not release it. Brennan laid the toddler down for a nap in the den while he joined the women on the patio for lunch.

Although Charis kept trying to needle Elle, he admired the way his wife chose to ignore her.

Later that evening, Elle surprised him by making herself comfortable on his lap. "Your daughter is precious."

"She is a sweetheart. I hope Charis didn't get on your nerves too much."

Shaking her head, Elle replied, "No, she didn't. Pookie and Muffin kept giving her a hard time. It helped that your mother decided not to come over after all." Kissing him, she asked, "Are you really interested in this movie?"

Cautiously, he replied, "No, not too interested. Why?"

She started to undo his shirt. "I was thinking we could go to bed early." Her eyes were full of meaning.

"Let's go upstairs," Brennan murmured huskily.

Trembling, she held on to his hand, the mere touch sending a warming shiver through her.

In the bedroom, Brennan claimed her lips as he crushed her to him. Elle matched him kiss for kiss. When she finally had the strength to pull away, she did so long enough to remove her clothes.

Brennan did the same. When they were both naked, he picked her up and carried her to bed. They made love slowly and through most of the night.

In the afterglow, Elle fell asleep in his arms.

The next morning, they had breakfast together on the patio.

Elle poured him a glass of orange juice. "Honey, I was thinking about something. We should decorate one of the bedrooms for Lauren."

Brennan laid down the newspaper he'd been reading. "You want to fix up a room for Lauren?"

She laughed. "Yes. That's what I said. She's your daughter, and I want her to be comfortable here."

"What brought all this on?" he asked.

"Seeing you with her yesterday. You really are a wonderful father. It's important for you to spend as much time as you can with her."

He reached over and took her hand. "You are wonderful, Elle, and I'm so glad to have you back."

Smiling, she said, "It's good to be back."

Chapter Fourteen

Elle spent Memorial Day working on the tour schedule for the performing artist known simply as Deacon. She'd been at her desk since eight that morning.

When she heard someone enter the office, she glanced up from her computer. Frowning, Elle asked, "What are you doing here?"

Charis dropped the stack of wallpaper samples she had been carrying onto the cherry-and-glass desk, then removed her sunglasses. "You're decorating Lauren's room, aren't you? Brennan mentioned it on the phone yesterday."

Leaning back in her chair, Elle wondered if Charis was baiting her. "What does it have to do with you?"

Making herself at home in one of the visitor chairs, Charis replied, "Well, I know my little girl better than anyone, and I know what she likes. That being the case, I came up with a wonderful idea. I'll go with you and Brennan to help."

Elle's medium brown eyes flashed with outrage. "We don't need your help."

"I wasn't asking," Charis stated coldly. "Lauren is *my* daughter."

"I'm all too well aware of that." Elle's tone was curt. "However, this is not your house—it's mine."

"This house belongs to Brennan."

"What's going on here?"

Both women looked toward the door. Brennan was standing there, wearing a look of irritation on his face.

"We were discussing Lauren's room," Elle announced. "Charis wants to help us decorate. I told her it wasn't necessary. We're very capable of picking out paint and wallpaper. Not to mention furnishings."

"I was explaining to your wife that I know my daughter's likes and dislikes. We want Lauren to feel comfortable over here."

"It's really not too hard a task to pick out stuff for a baby," Elle argued.

"I want Lauren's room to be an expression of her personality."

Leaning back in her chair, Elle inquired, "Brennan, what do you think?"

He gave a slight shrug. "Maybe Charis is right. She should go with us. We do want Lauren to love her room."

Elle's body stiffened and she sat up straight. "For goodness sake, she's a baby, Brennan."

"Lauren has her own personality," Charis interjected.

"I don't believe this," Elle muttered, rolling her eyes heavenward.

Brennan held up his hand. "Let's not make this a big deal. Charis will just give her opinion, that's all."

"Whatever!" Snatching her purse, Elle stood. "Let's just get this over with," she snapped.

She was silent during the drive to Rodeo Drive in Beverly Hills. Elle was furious with Brennan. How could he let this woman come into their home and decorate?

As usual, Charis prattled on. . . .

"I've always loved the way the master suite was designed. With you right there for Lauren—"

"Excuse me?" Elle interjected. She turned around in her seat. "What are you babbling about now?"

"I'm talking about the nursery."

"Lauren's room will be the one next to ours."

Charis stared out of the window. "I really won't feel comfortable leaving Lauren with you and Brennan overnight if she's going to be sleeping down the hall."

"Where does she sleep at your mother's house?" Elle asked.

"I don't think it's really any of your business."

"I'm sure she's not in the room with you. She's probably not even on the same floor. Doesn't she sleep with the nanny?"

"No! Lauren has her own room."

"Who's closer to her? You or the nanny?"

Charis didn't answer.

"She will sleep in the room next to ours and that's final." Elle faced the front. She was thankful Brennan hadn't gone against her decision this time.

Inside the huge baby department of Bloodstone's department store, Brennan pulled her to an empty area and asked, "What's wrong with you, Elle?"

Keeping her voice low, she replied, "How dare you humiliate me like that! Just get away from me."

"Will you stop acting like a child? Look, I'm trying

to make the best of a bad situation. Could you help me out, please?"

Elle glared at him in response. She was so angry right now she could spit nails. Brennan had actually sided with Charis.

Standing alone in the middle of the department, surrounded by cribs, accessories, and other baby items, Elle felt her chest tighten and her breathing become difficult. Coming here had been a mistake. Feeling dizzy, Elle rushed toward the elevator.

Brennan had a strong suspicion that he'd really screwed up this time. Elle was furious with him. She'd refused to talk to him or assist Charis in any way. Not that Charis wanted her help. He was grateful when the shopping spree was over.

After dinner, she'd gone straight to their bedroom. He waited a couple of hours before joining her. As he opened the door, Brennan prayed she would be over her anger.

He could tell she wasn't as soon as he walked into the room, the tension was that thick. Brennan didn't say a word to her; instead, he jumped into the shower.

When he was done, he crawled into bed and laid beside his wife. "Good night, sweetheart."

Elle didn't respond.

Brennan propped himself up on one arm. "Elle, I'm sorry. I can't take this silent treatment any longer. Let's talk about whatever is bothering you."

"Charis Wentworth is bothering me. She had no right to come into our house and decorate Lauren's bedroom. This is *our* home. Not hers."

Brennan sat up in bed. "You let her take over, Elle.

I thought two adult women would be able to come to a compromise. Obviously, I was wrong.''

Elle sat up, too. ''She shouldn't have had anything to do with this, Brennan.''

''Lauren is her daughter. I could see if we were talking about our children.''

Her arms folded across her chest, Elle frowned. *''I see.* I'm only your wife. Lauren and I will have no relationship, is that it?''

''That's not what I'm saying.''

''I don't want to talk about this anymore. We're getting nowhere.''

''This is not over. I want to settle this tonight.''

''It's settled, Brennan. I'm not going to have anything to do with that room.''

''That's childish,'' Brennan uttered. ''I expected more of you, Elle.''

''I really don't care what you expect. I've said what I had to say.'' She eased down into the bed and turned her back to him. ''Good night.''

Brennan sighed in frustration. How in the world was he going to make this work?

After two weeks of paint, wallpaper, and a string of deliverymen, the room was finally finished. Although she'd vowed never to set foot into Lauren's bedroom, Elle couldn't resist a peek.

Surveying the room, she had to admit it was beautifully decorated. Charis had chosen a daisy theme throughout. A delightful yellow daisy print on a cornflower blue background covered the twin-size bed. The wooden-slat headboard featured a cutout design of a flower stem and a single leaf, and was hand-painted in yellow.

Next to the bed stood a five-drawer nightstand with a unique design painted in white. A rice-paper shade in the shape of a flower adorned the top.

Elle picked up the daisy alarm clock. "This room has everything." Returning it back to the lattice-wall shelf, she uttered, "I was going to do the room in Winnie the Pooh. *What was I thinking?*"

On her way out, she ran her fingers across the picket-fence toy box. It still bothered Elle that Brennan had sided with Charis. When it came to Charis, they would never agree, she had come to realize. He'd accused her of acting childish when Elle had decided to back out of the project.

Gritting her teeth, she strode past the three-story wooden dollhouse that Charis had insisted Lauren had to have.

It was a room—a simple room. It was over and done with, yet Elle couldn't let the matter drop. She felt betrayed, and it hurt.

Chapter Fifteen

Today was Muffin and Steve's wedding day. Despite the tension between Elle and her husband, they both tried to give the appearance of a happy couple. They had not spoken to each other in almost three weeks, but it hadn't lessened Elle's attraction for Brennan. She thought he looked quite handsome in his dark navy suit and red tie. He wore a small red rose in his upper left pocket.

Brennan greeted all the guests warmly as they entered the church. Every now and then he would stop by and check on her. She would respond, "I'm fine." Brennan would then move on. Elle hated the gulf between them. She didn't want to fight with him anymore—instead, she craved the feel of his arms around her, his lips on hers . . . she gave a soft sigh.

Elle felt her temper rise as soon as she caught sight of Charis on Randall's arm. He escorted her to the row across from where Elle was sitting. What could he possibly see in that woman? she wanted to know.

The chapel was filled mostly with family members and a few close friends. Muffin's brother-in-law, Dr. Hugh Gaines, escorted her into the church.

Her wedding attire, a two-piece Valentino, was an eggshell color with long sleeves, a round neck, and a skirt that graced the tops of her knees.

Immediately after the service ended, the newly married couple walked hand in hand out of the tiny oceanfront chapel in Pacific Palisades.

Muffin and Steve climbed into a stretch limo, which drove them the short distance to the Lake Estate. The guests followed in their own cars.

Elle and Brennan were seated at a table with Jordan and her brothers. Elle enjoyed the stories being passed around about their childhood. Although Jordan was the only girl out of five children, her brothers absolutely adored her.

Elle listened as Brennan and Jordan fondly recalled an incident that happened when they were younger.

Laughing, Brennan said, "Honey, wait until you meet her brother, Damien. He's the one who has always made Jordan crazy."

"He used to rent me out for dates."

Looking from one to the other, Elle asked, "Really?"

Laughing, Jordan nodded. "I think he made fifty dollars one summer until I realized what was going on. It broke my heart because I thought that particular boy liked me."

"That's so mean," Elle murmured.

Holding up his champagne flute, Brennan said, "To the good ol' days . . ."

After his toast, Jordan made one of her own. Elle took a sip of the sparkling golden liquid in her glass.

Brennan winked at her playfully, but she only stared

back. Elle was determined not to let him gloss over the situation. He'd really hurt her by his actions. Forgiveness would not come that easily.

When he didn't get the response he'd hoped for, Brennan stood and said, "I'm going to say hello to a few people. I'll be back shortly."

Elle nodded.

"Are things okay between the two of you?"

"We're fine," she said. Elle wasn't sure Jordan believed her, but she let the matter drop.

Leaning over, Jordan whispered, "I'm so glad Muffin and my dad finally got married. I feel like I've been waiting a long time for this day to happen."

"You really like her, don't you?" Elle asked.

Nodding, she stated, "Muffin's been in my life since I was thirteen. She's come close to being the only mother I've known. I love her dearly."

"She's a sweet lady."

"Yes, she is. And she's a saint for putting up with Daddy all of these years. I don't know if I could have waited on a man this long." Jordan gave a short laugh. "At the rate I'm going, I'm going to be alone for a long time. I'm too picky."

"It just takes the right man."

"Well, whenever I find him, I hope I'm going to like him."

"You will," Elle assured her. "I know it."

"What are you two beautiful ladies laughing about?"

Elle glanced up to find a tall slender man standing in front of them.

Squealing with delight, Jordan rushed to her feet. "Damien! You made it. Daddy's going to be so happy." She tossed Elle a look. "I almost forgot. You haven't met Brennan's wife."

He gave her a quick once-over. "No, I haven't."

"This is Elle. Elle, this is my brother, Damien. He lives in Raleigh, North Carolina."

She smiled and held out her hand. "It's nice to meet you."

Shaking her hand, Damien smiled. "You, too. Brennan's a very lucky man."

I just wish he thought so. "Thank you."

Brennan sought them out. He and his cousin embraced happily, then talked for a while. Every now and then he would glance over at her. Finally, he ended his conversation with Damien and approached the table. Brennan sat down next to Elle.

Standing up, Jordan said, "I'm going to catch up with Jensen. I'll be back shortly."

Elle nodded. "Okay."

"Have I told you how beautiful you look today, sweetheart?"

She stared at the water glass on the table. Elle couldn't look at him right now. She wasn't about to give in so easily. "Thank you."

"Are you still mad at me?" Brennan whispered in her ear. His lips tickled her ear.

It was having the desired effect on her, because Elle started to smile. "Yes, I am."

"I don't want you to be mad at me anymore." He kissed her cheek. "I hate when you're sad." Brennan's lips grazed her ears once more. "Let's make up."

Her body trembled in response.

"Brennan . . ." Elle closed her eyes.

"I miss you."

She opened her eyes and confessed, "I'm glad, because I've missed you so much."

"Show me," he said huskily.

Elle's eyes grew wide. "What?"

"Kiss me."

Flushed, she glanced around. "Brennan, there are people all over the place. What's gotten into you?"

"It's just a kiss. I'm not asking you to make love to me on the table."

"I've never known you to be one for public displays."

"Just one kiss."

Leaning into him, Elle kissed him softly on the lips.

"Look at her. Elle may think she's won, but little does she know that I don't intend to give up without a fight." Charis glared across the room to where Elle was sitting with Brennan. "I really can't believe he actually married the witch."

"Charis, get ahold of yourself," Randall whispered. He glanced around to see if anyone could overhear them.

"There's no reason for Brennan to continue their farce of a marriage. The baby died."

Shaking his head, Randall was disgusted. "How can you be so heartless?"

"I've got to find a way to get him back."

"Excuse me?"

"I've got to get Brennan back," Charis announced with fierce determination. "I will not allow Lauren to grow up without her father."

"That won't happen with Brennan. He's not going to leave his wife, Charis. Even you should know him better than that."

"Brennan may stay with her because she's making him feel guilty over their son's death. Elle's playing on his emotions, and I'm going to stop her. She won't get away with this, Randall. Their only tie was that baby, and he's gone. Lauren and I will always be a big part of Brennan's life. And at one time, he loved me. I've just got to remind him of that."

"I think you're making a mistake, Charis. If you don't end this game you're playing, you are going to lose everything."

"I don't agree. The odds are in my favor."

"How do you figure that?"

"Lauren is his firstborn, and it drives Elle crazy. Especially since her own child is gone. She's so jealous of their relationship and his relationship with me."

Randall shook his head in disagreement. "I don't believe that."

"It's true." Charis laughed with glee. "You should have seen how angry she was when Brennan agreed to let me decorate Lauren's room. She practically had a tantrum."

"It looks like they've gotten past it," Randall observed.

Charis followed his gaze. "For the moment maybe." Kissing him on the cheek, she whispered, "Just watch this."

Grabbing her by the arm, Randall demanded, "What are you going to do?"

Snatching her arm away, she replied, "Tear Brennan away from that clinging vine he calls a wife. I'm sure he needs a break from all that whining she does."

Charis crossed the room in quick strides. "Wasn't it a beautiful wedding?"

"Yes, it was," Elle agreed. "What do you want?"

Plastering on a fake smile, she answered, "I need to borrow Brennan for a bit. I want to have the photographer take pictures of Lauren, her father, and me. Then we can put them in her room."

She waited for the explosion that was sure to come but was disappointed.

Elle didn't even blink. Instead, she smiled and said, "I think it's a good idea. Lauren should have some pictures of her father."

"How very gracious of you," Charis said tightly.

Brennan kissed the back of Elle's hand before releasing it. "I'll be back shortly."

Giving Elle a wicked grin, Charis said, "I'll give him back once I'm done with him."

Pookie sat down beside Elle. "Where's that handsome husband of yours?"

"He's taking pictures with Charis somewhere. Family photos for Lauren." She tried to pretend she was calmer than she actually felt. Try as she might, she didn't like the idea of Brennan being alone with that woman. Elle knew exactly what Charis was capable of.

"Honey, you'd better listen to Pookie. Go find your man. That Wentworth gal is nothing but trouble. I wouldn't give her an inch, because she's greedy enough to take the entire foot." Pookie downed the last of her champagne and reached for another as the waiter made another pass through the guests.

"I have faith in my husband. He knows how to conduct himself."

Smiling, Pookie nodded. "All right now." She took another sip of champagne. "You're so good for Brennan."

"I think so."

"You are. My nephew is a good man. Maybe naive at times, but a good man nonetheless."

After finishing her drink, Pookie strolled over to the platform and reached for one of the microphones. Dressed in a stunning ankle-length dress with a high slit, she struck a pose as cameras whirred and flashed around the room.

Gesturing to the band, Pookie began to sway as they played. She broke out into a song.

Elle smiled when Jordan returned to the table and sat down.

"She has a beautiful voice," Elle whispered.

"Pookie can sing up a storm. You should hear her and Brennan singing together. They sound heavenly."

Elle's eyes searched the room. She didn't see Brennan anywhere. She wasn't worried though, because when the reception was over, her husband would be going home with her. At least Charis couldn't sabotage that.

"What's your hurry? Little wifey can't bear to be alone for a few minutes?" Charis wrapped her arms around Brennan.

Removing her hands, he replied, "Charis, drop it. You wanted pictures—you got them."

"But we didn't take any as a family. It would be nice for Lauren to have at least one photo of her mother and father together."

Brennan growled in frustration. "Fine. Let's take a picture so that I can get back to my wife."

Charis hung on to him for dear life. He counted the minutes, praying for this session to come to an end.

Finally they were done. Brennan walked away without preamble.

Charis called out to him. "Wait . . ."

"I need to return to my wife. She's been very understanding about the pictures—"

She laughed harshly. "I can't believe it! You're being led by the nose by a woman."

He glared at her. "What do you want?"

"I just got a brilliant idea. Why don't you come by the house later and read Lauren a bedtime story?"

"Sure. Elle and I would love to do that."

"I don't want your wife in my home. I thought I'd made that clear."

"And I thought I'd made it clear that I will not allow you to continue to disrespect my wife. Elle has done nothing to you."

"She's made it abundantly clear that she doesn't want me and Lauren in your life."

"Elle told you that?"

"Not in so many words. I can see it in her face and the way she talks to me. Lauren doesn't need to be around two women who obviously can't get along. I've tried."

"So has Elle."

"She's your wife, so I expect you to defend her, but you really should remove your blinders. Elle is not the woman you think she is."

"I'm going to join my wife."

Catching Elle's attention, Brennan winked. He crossed the room in quick strides. After kissing her on the cheek, he sat down in the chair next to her, saying, "I didn't mean to stay away so long."

"I'm fine. Jordan's been keeping me company."

"Ready to go home?" he asked hopefully.

"I am." Elle gazed across the tent to where Charis was standing. "Let's get out of here."

Looking up at her husband, she gave him a bright smile.

Brennan's body ached for her touch. His feelings for Elle were intensifying, and he was powerless.

Chapter Sixteen

A week passed, then another. There hadn't been any word from Charis, and Elle was grateful for that tiny blessing. She knew it was because Brennan had been in New York for the past week and a half. They were getting ready to debut the new Advantage fragrance line.

He had spoken with Elle an hour earlier from the plane and was due home any time now. As soon as she'd heard from Brennan, she'd left work early to prepare a romantic dinner for the two of them.

It had been a task getting Robert out of the kitchen. Elle had finally succeeded in getting him and Melina to take in a movie and go to dinner, her treat, afterward. She wanted to have the entire house to themselves.

Three hours later, she greeted Brennan at the door with a glass of wine. Elle marveled at the way his eyes melted her composure until she could hardly put two coherent words together.

He joined her in the living room, leaving his luggage in the foyer. They sat looking at each other across the coffee table, the lights from scented candles flickering around the room.

"Where's Melina?" Brennan asked.

"I gave her and Robert the night off." Elle gave him a sexy smile. "I thought we needed a night alone. Totally alone."

Brennan sipped his wine. "I agree." His voice was husky. "Making love to you is all I've been able to think about."

Elle couldn't breathe or think right now. Every part of her turned to liquid heat. She closed her eyes and wet her lips.

Her thick lashes lifted and Elle gazed into Brennan's eyes. The heat in their brown depths sent bolts of desire shooting through them both.

"Why are you sitting over there?" he asked. "Come here." Brennan set the wineglass on the coffee table.

Elle did as he wanted. She dropped down beside him.

He pulled her into his arms, causing Elle to slip weightless as a cloud into their own little world. Brennan kissed her.

Elle moved her lips under his. Everything felt so right between them. Her fingers began to unbutton his shirt. "I want you." Her voice was low, husky, and barely discernible over the beating of her own heart. She pressed her lips to his, wanting more of his kisses.

Brennan's lips dragged reluctantly from hers. "You are too good for me. I don't deserve you, Elle."

"Why do you say that?"

"Because you're so patient with me. I've come into this marriage with a lot of . . . a lot of baggage."

Smiling, she stroked his cheek. "I love you, Brennan. Haven't you figured that out yet?"

"I've known for a while," Brennan admitted. "I just don't deserve your love. It's wasted on me."

"Why do you say tha—"

"No more questions," he murmured. Brennan covered her mouth with his. His hands stroked the sweep of her body. He had a talent for attending to detail, and Elle writhed beneath it all. She was totally oblivious to everything except where he touched and where he kissed.

When Elle felt she could stand it no longer, Brennan stopped. Running his fingers through her hair, he murmured, "I want to make love to you right now, right here." He caressed her, touching her all over.

She was breathless with anticipation. Her head lolled back in languid submission. Elle looked up at him, her eyes dark with heat and her breath coming out ragged.

They were good together, she had to admit. More than good. Only when Elle was with Brennan had she ever felt so fullfilled . . . so complete.

Lying beneath a blanket on the carpeted floor, Brennan handed her a piece of paper.

"Did you write me another song?"

"I was inspired in New York. Alone in my suite at the Plaza Hotel."

"Will you sing it to me?"

Elle couldn't stop her flow of tears as she listened to his words. Brennan's voice lulled her into a world where she felt loved. . . . She opened her eyes. He had his eyes closed, but it didn't matter. Her heart overflowed with happiness.

He was falling in love with her. Of that she was sure. This was what couples were supposed to feel in their marriages. The ethereal aspects of love and the melding of separate spirits. Brennan probably hadn't realized it himself, but Elle could feel it. When he finished singing, she kissed him deeply.

"Oh, Brennan . . . you are such a sweetheart. I love it. You are a great singer and a wonderful songwriter. Don't you miss it?"

"Sometimes. Now, back to the song." He pulled out a plastic case. "I recorded it so that you could hear it as much as you like." Brennan handed her a compact disc.

Excited, Elle threw her arms around him. "Thank you so much. It means a lot to me."

Brennan grew very serious. "I know that this is not the kind of marriage you had in mind, but I give you my word that you will want for nothing, Elle. I will give you the world."

"It's not the world I'm after."

"What is it you want then?"

Elle placed a hand to his chest. "I want your heart."

"I don't know if I can give you that," he whispered against her neck.

Brennan's warm breath tickled. She shivered in delicious anticipation of what would come later. "Are you at least willing to try?" Elle hadn't meant to push, but she couldn't stop herself. She loved Brennan beyond reason.

He smiled at her then. "Lets just take this one day at a time."

"I'll agree to that," Elle responded. "I just want you to keep an open mind." She stood up and held out her hand to him. "Let's shower and get dressed. I practically had to fight Robert to gain entry to the kitchen, so we'd better eat."

"You cooked?"

"Don't look so surprised, Brennan. I can cook, you know. My mother taught all of us to cook and keep a decent house." Taking him by the hand, Elle led him to the dining room. "Tonight is going to be a night we won't forget," she promised.

The candles placed all over the bedroom cast a soft romantic glow. In the candlelight, Brennan watched Elle as she moved to the antique dressing table, where she sat and removed the barrette that had been holding her hair back.

Brennan thought he'd never seen anyone so beautiful in his life than Elle was at that moment. He lay there watching her graceful motions as she brushed her long tresses.

Finally she put the brush down next to a matching comb and hand mirror. Brennan's heart started a hard and steady thumping when Elle pushed to her feet and turned. She looked so sexy, she made his chest ache.

The firm mattress on the king-size bed didn't shift under her weight as she joined him. Elle turned off the lamp before crawling under the covers.

Brennan slid his arm beneath her head. "Sweetheart," he whispered. He pulled her toward him. He held her close and savored the feel of her body nestled against him.

He kissed her hungrily. It was as if he wanted to possess all of her, inside and out. Elle moaned, and he could sense her urgency. Desire became a wild animal within him, clawing for release.

Brennan took a moment to feast on the sight of her. Elle was more beautiful than his most inspired imaginings. Brennan traced the length of her spine with his hand.

She arched convulsively against him, urging him to douse the fire that burned within.

Sometime later, they clung to each other, their breathing ragged. Their lovemaking didn't end the white-hot explosion of passion that existed between them. It would take a lifetime to do that.

Her skin hot and slick, Elle wrapped her arm around Brennan and snuggled closer against him. Losing himself in her warmth, Brennan slept.

Treach was performing in Dallas two days later, and Elle flew out for the concert. She'd arranged for an early radio interview and he was scheduled to perform on the morning show on channel 56. Although she would only be gone for one night, Elle missed her husband. She'd pleaded with him to join her, and Brennan had promised to try and join her as soon as he could.

Her cell phone began to vibrate. Elle pulled it out of her purse. "Hello."

It was Brennan, and he was upset. "I've got to stay here, sweetheart."

"Your father, right?" Elle glanced at her watch. They would have to be leaving soon.

"Look, it's only for the night. I'll see you tomorrow."

Elle hid her disappointment. "I'm still going to miss you. Even if it is for one night."

"I'm going to miss you, too. I'm tired of being away from you. I told Father before we got married that I wanted to cut back, but I guess he's not listening." He sighed loudly. "Enjoy the concert."

"Brennan, I love you."

"I know," he replied softly.

"I've got to go, but I'll see you tomorrow, okay?" Elle clicked off. Maybe she shouldn't have declared her love like that, but it was too late now. Besides, Brennan needed to hear it. He needed to know just how much he meant to her.

"I don't want to sit up at the hospital while Regis gives birth," Brennan argued. "Besides that, it's the Fourth of July."

"Fine. What about after she has the baby? Will you go with me then? It's not like we were doing anything special today. You didn't want to go to Jillian's house."

He tried to return his attention to the book in his lap. "I'm not crazy about hospitals. You'll see the baby when it comes home."

"What's wrong with you?" Elle demanded.

"Sweetheart, you're going to have to grow up one day soon and leave the family nest."

"Excuse me?"

"I don't intend to spend all of my time with your family. We don't need to drive to Riverside every Sunday or every single holiday. We don't need to gather at the hospital for every birth. I want us to make our own traditions."

"And we will, Brennan. But my family is very important to me. They are so much a part of who I am—I won't give them up."

"I'm not asking you to do that. Just don't expect me to be a part of all that nonsense, either."

"It's not nonsense." Fury marring her features, Elle snapped, "I really don't like this part of you." She ran out of the room.

Brennan assumed she would cool off after a while, but when two hours passed and there was no sign of her, he grew worried.

For one painful, heartstopping moment, Brennan thought Elle had left the house. But when he went upstairs to their bedroom, he heard the water running in the master bath. Brennan crept across the hardwood floor and peeked inside the bathroom. Elle was in the tub.

Moisture beaded her mocha-hued shoulders and slender throat. Her dark hair had been put in an upswept style. Eyes closed, Elle leaned back with her head resting against the rim of the garden bathtub.

As he often did, Brennan found it hard to believe that Elle was really his. That she was his wife. She didn't stir, except for the slight rise and fall of her chest as she breathed softly.

"Sweetheart?" he whispered.

Elle's lips formed a smile, encouraging him. She wasn't still upset with him.

"The bath looks inviting." Brennan couldn't dismiss this sensation of fullness, of a heart that threatened to explode with emotion any moment, every time he looked at her.

"Why don't you join me?" she asked huskily. Opening her eyes, Elle added, "The water's still nice and hot."

Brennan couldn't control the fierce yearning for her touch or the constant hunger for her. "I'm sorry for upsetting you."

"I'm sorry, too. I just want you to understand that my family and I are very close. We've always been this way. I just can't change overnight."

"Honey, I know that. I don't expect you to change— just don't try to force me into changing who I am, either.

My family isn't a close one. To be perfectly honest, I can take them or leave them."

"I'm going to change that for you, Brennan. I'm going to show you what it's like to be a part of a loving family. . . ."

Chapter Seventeen

Brennan drove over to the Wentworth estate to pick up Lauren. She was going to spend the weekend with him and Elle.

Mrs. Tally Wentworth was standing in the foyer when he arrived, looking as sullen as always. When the housekeeper disappeared to find Charis, the woman stated coldly, "You are a disappointment to me, Brennan. How could you treat my daughter like this?"

"What are you talking about, Mrs. Wentworth?"

"She gives birth to your daughter and you run off and marry someone else. Charis deserved much better from you."

"The woman I married was also carrying my child. Everyone seems to forget that." His gaze dared her to say what had to be going through her mind right then.

Charis joined them. "Brennan, darling, let's go into the living room. Ariel's getting Lauren ready and they should be down shortly." She glared at her mother while taking his hand and leading Brennan over to a floral love seat.

The look on his face prompted her to ask, "Did Mother say something to upset you?"

He shook his head no. "She's just trying to look out for you, I suppose."

"My mother thinks you should have married me."

"I know," Brennan answered with an impersonal nod. "She made that much clear."

"I still love you," Charis said softly.

He shook his head in dismay. "Don't do this, Charis. Elle and I are married. It's too late for us."

Pushing stray tendrils of hair away from her cheek, Charis set her chin in a stubborn line. "But you don't love her. I can see it in your eyes." She eyed him. "What happened to us?"

"It doesn't bear talking about." Brennan didn't think the argument that would surely follow was worth the headache.

Ariel descended the stairs carrying Lauren. When she reached the bottom of the stairs, she put the toddler down.

"Do you ever think about me?"

Brennan picked up Lauren when she ran over to him. "No, not really."

"Look at us. We're a family. Surely you can't deny that."

"Lauren is my daughter and Elle is my wife. *We* are a family."

For a moment a faraway look darkened Charis's eyes. She blinked it away. Pouting, she said, "I never thought you would be so cruel. I know we've had our problems, but I never knew you hated me."

"I don't hate you, Charis. I just don't trust you. Without trust, there can't be anything. Just do me a favor and stop trying to insinuate yourself into my life. I intend to be a father to Lauren, but that's it. You and I will have no relationship outside of the bond we share as parents. Understand?''

Charis cringed. ''You will one day regret those words. Your marriage is not going to last, Brennan. We both know it. I'm not going to sit around waiting for you, either. One day I'm going to get married and my husband will be the one Lauren calls Daddy. Remember that.''

His expression was a mask of stone. ''My daughter will know who I am. I intend to make sure of that, Charis.'' It bothered him to think of Lauren calling another man Daddy. ''I intend to take on an active role in her life, whether you are married or not.''

''No matter how you try to fix it up, the fact remains that you will only be a part-time father.''

Brennan stood up with Lauren in his arms. ''I'll have her home on Sunday by five.''

''Are you sure this is the way you want things?'' Charis questioned. ''What if Elle can't give you another child? Have you thought about that?''

He was getting angrier by the minute. Charis had always known how to push his buttons. Frowning in exasperation, Brennan made his way to the door. ''I'm not going to have this discussion.''

From behind him, Charis couldn't resist one last barb. ''You may not want to discuss it, but you should at least think about what I've said. Lauren may be your only chance at being a father.''

Storming out of the house, Brennan worried that Charis could be right. He and Elle had been trying for a month to get pregnant. So far, they hadn't been able to conceive.

Elle worried that something was wrong with her, because she'd gotten pregnant so easily before. Nothing Brennan said could convince her otherwise.

Elle faxed over the copy of the last press release that needed to go out.

Malcolm strolled out of his office. "Hey, I thought you'd gone home a long time ago."

"No, there were some things I needed to take care of."

"Oh, I left a packet on my desk for you. It's the photos for Tracy Carroll. They're going to look great on her album cover."

"I'll get it before I leave."

Fifteen minutes later, Elle entered Malcolm's office to pick up the packet off his desk. While in there, her eyes inadvertently strayed to the photo on the wall of Brennan and Malcolm.

Her husband looked so happy in the picture. Elle suspected his first love had always been music. Brennan was forever hanging around the Jupiter offices. She'd once joked that he should apply for a position there.

Elle had a feeling that Brennan hadn't been as happy or fulfilled as he had been during his singing career. She knew he missed it.

Maybe one day she would sit down with him and suggest that he leave the company. It would be his decision, however. Elle wasn't sure Brennan could ever walk away from his father.

* * *

The following Sunday, Elle drove out to Riverside. She and Brennan argued about it for an hour before he finally relented to come with her.

"You're going to have a good time."

"Elle, I was content with staying home alone with you. You know I have to leave for France tomorrow morning." His tone contained a vague hint of disapproval.

The corner of her mouth twisted with exasperation. "We'll just leave right after dinner, okay?"

All the way to Riverside, Brennan's mouth was set in annoyance. Elle wished he'd stayed at home with the mood he was in. She had no idea why he hated going to her mother's house so much. Her family was nothing like his—they were loving and just fun to be around. Elle wanted him to feel as comfortable around her family as she did. They were his family now.

As soon as they arrived, Elle ran into the house and grabbed her mother. "Mama, I missed you so much."

"I missed you, too." Amanda looked past her daughter. "Hello, Brennan. Come on in."

"Hello, everyone," he called out.

"Girl, why is he so stiff?" Allura whispered to Elle. "He acts like he's afraid of us."

"He's just not real comfortable around you all. Brennan knows that you guys aren't crazy about him. I'm hoping to change all that."

"I don't think that's it," Allura stated. "I think he's just a stuffed shirt."

Elle elbowed her sister. "Leave my husband alone." She walked over to the corner where Brennan was standing. Pulling him by the arm, she led him through the house and to the patio. "Most everyone is outside." She glanced up at him, trying to make him smile.

Brennan already looked bored. Sighing in frustration, she said, "You could at least put forth an effort to be friendly."

"I'm here. Be satisfied with that. Just don't expect me to jump into your little happy-family routine."

The cynicism of his remark grated on her nerves. This had been a very bad idea, Elle decided.

Brennan was glad to finally be back home. As soon as they set foot in their bedroom, Elle questioned him on his actions. "My brothers tried to include you in the basketball game and you refused. Nyle tried to get you to play spades, and you turned him down, too. The only person you really talked to was Chandra," she accused. "Why won't you let people get close to you? You live behind a wall, and I don't understand it."

Brennan removed his shirt. Dropping down on the edge of the bed, he bent to remove his shoes and socks. "Elle, you don't know much about my life. You don't have a clue."

She sat down beside him. "Then why won't you tell me? Honey, please talk to me."

He looked over at her, studying her face. "What do you want to know? Do you really want to know what my privileged life was like?"

"Of course I do." Elle took his hand in hers. "I want to know everything about you."

As Brennan talked about his childhood, his thoughts traveled back to a time when he was about nine or ten years old. A friend from school had been playing with his collection of cars that Brennan's father had given him for his birthday. Missing yet another birthday party for his son, he'd come home two days later from a business trip and presented an armload of gifts to him.

Brennan had accepted them without emotion.

"I'd love to have one of these," the boy had sighed.

"I would gladly give them all to you," Brennan had told his friend. "If you could give me something you have."

"You can have anything I have," the boy had answered immediately.

"No, this is something you can't give me," Brennan had said sadly.

"I'll give you anything you want. Just tell me what you want and I'll give it to you."

"I want two parents just like yours," Brennan had told him firmly. "I want parents who love me and who love each other."

"What happened when you said that?" Elle asked.

"My friend handed the car back to me without another word."

Brennan grew quiet, caught up in his painful memories.

Elle touched him lightly. "I'm sure your parents loved you, or maybe they didn't know how to love you."

"I don't think it's because they didn't know how. I just don't think they cared about anything outside of money. Despite all the gifts they bought me, the one thing I wanted most from them was love and their attention. When I couldn't get that, I figured they felt I wasn't worthy of love."

"You don't believe that now, do you?"

Brennan's silence was her answer.

He stood up briskly, saying, "I need a drink."

"Do you want me to wait up?" Elle asked.

"No, don't worry about waiting up for me. You should get some rest."

"You need your rest as well," she pointed out. "You're the one leaving in the morning."

"I can sleep on my plane though." Brennan disappeared from the room as quickly as he could.

Elle was asleep when he returned to the master bedroom. As quietly as he could manage, Brennan undressed and eased into bed. She turned on her side, her back to him. He moved closer, throwing his arm across her waist.

Brennan closed his eyes as he relished the feel of Elle's body. He needed her warmth to melt the ice around his heart. Only she could never know.

He'd let Elle get too close to him tonight. Brennan couldn't handle that. He was going to have to put some distance between the two of them. Thank God, he was leaving on a business trip.

Brennan did a lot of thinking during the night hours, the image of Elle burning into his mind. There were so many things he wanted to say to her, but a lifetime of restraint held him back.

Chapter Eighteen

With Brennan out of town, the house always seemed even larger. What in the world could Brennan have been thinking when he bought this huge estate? Was he merely trying to keep up with his parents? Or had it been expected since he was a man of great wealth?

As usual, Elle found herself returning to her favorite place in the entire house—the library. Like her, Brennan was a lover of books. He had a vast collection of first-edition copies of books by Langston Hughes, Zora Neale Hurston, and James Baldwin.

Elle scanned shelf after shelf in search of something to read. She found a copy of *The Dark Child* by Camara Laye. The doorbell sounded before she'd made a decision. Placing the book back on the shelf, she turned and headed to the front entrance. "Who in the world could this be?" she wondered aloud.

Melina and Robert had gone to run errands. Elle was alone and wasn't expecting anyone.

The doorbell rang a second time. She stole a peek

outside through a small window to the side of the door. Elle threw open the door, a smile lighting her face. "Pookie. Muffin. Come on in. I'm so glad to see you."

"We knew Brennan was away on business, so we thought we'd come keep you company for a bit," Muffin explained. "I told Pookie we should have called first. Please forgive our lack of manners."

Elle laughed. "It's fine. I'm happy to see you both."

They gathered in the den. "Would you ladies like something to drink?" Elle asked. "I could get you some iced tea."

"I'll take one," Pookie announced. "I'm feeling kind of thirsty." She scanned Elle from head to toe and grinned. "Girl, you getting some bragging rights. . . ." Pookie murmured as she pointed to Elle's hips. "Looks like you're putting back on some of the weight you lost."

Elle burst into laughter. "Pookie, you're something else."

"Yes, she is indeed," Muffin agreed. "It's her unique view of the world that I adore most about her."

"I'm just cute," Pookie announced. "And people hate me for it. Take Lizbeth for example. Her biggest problem with me is that I'm the prettier one. Everyone in the family always thought so."

Elle burst into another round of laughter.

Shaking her head, Muffin said, "Pookie is quite the character, isn't she?"

"Yes, she sure is," Elle agreed. "I'm so glad you two came by. I was bored out of my mind."

"It can be lonely in such a huge house." Elle sat on the arm of her sectional sofa.

"I love the house, but sometimes I feel so lost in it."

"Why don't you and Brennan sell this one? Get your-selves something smaller," Pookie suggested.

"After the way I carried on about the ring, I don't know if I should."

"What happened, dear?" Muffin asked.

Elle related the ring incident to Pookie and Muffin.

"Not everyone needs bigger, I suppose. That's what I'm always trying to tell Lizbeth. She thinks she's got to prove just how rich she is to the rest of the world in everything. Like some of the food she insists on eating. You have no idea what it really is. Give me some fried chicken and waffles, and I'm happy as a clam."

Elle shrugged. "I guess I just don't need a lot of things. I just want to be comfortable."

"My late husband, Max Worthington, was determined to give me the finest money could buy. All I wanted was his love. When he died, he left me with a lot of money, but I would gladly have been penniless just to see his charming smile one more time." She played with the five-carat diamond ring on her finger. "And now I have Steven. He's just as wonderful and just as loving, if not more."

"I just want Brennan's love. I really don't need any-thing else," Elle announced. "Money and security are nice, but it's love I want most."

"When will our nephew be back?" Pookie ques-tioned. "I wish Edward would stop sending him all around the world. He needs to remember that you and Brennan are still newlyweds."

"He's going to try and come home sometime tomor-row. His dad wants him to stay in the Paris office for yet another week, but Brennan says it's really not neces-sary. I'm so tempted to call Mr. Cunningham and tell him that my husband is nothing like him. Brennan actually likes spending time at home with me. I feel like we don't spend enough time together."

Muffin eyed Elle. "Dear, it's so obvious how much you love Brennan. I hope my darling nephew appreciates you."

Elle's smile was tight.

Elle was asleep when Brennan arrived home that night. In the morning, she saw his suitcase and jumped out of bed. She showered and quickly dressed, hoping to catch him at breakfast.

Melina poured her a glass of orange juice as soon as she entered the dining room.

"Thank you." Elle glanced into the kitchen. "Where's Brennan?"

"He left early this morning."

"He's gone already?" She was surprised. It was unusual for him to leave without at least saying hello. "Did he say where he was going?"

"His father called and requested an early morning meeting at the office." Changing the subject, she asked, "What would you like for breakfast, Mrs. Cunningham?"

"A ham-and-cheese omelette, please."

After breakfast, Elle called Malcolm to let him know she was going to work from home today. She spent most of her morning returning phone calls and sending out correspondence.

Shortly after noon, Elle drove over to Cunningham Lake Cosmetics.

Brennan was clearly surprised to see her. "What are you doing here?"

"Well, since I haven't seen you in a couple of weeks, I thought I'd take my handsome husband to lunch."

Brennan gazed into her eyes. "I appreciate the thought, but I have a lot of work to do. I'd planned on having something delivered."

She tried to hide her disappointment. "I want to talk to you. I miss you."

"I'll be home early this evening. I promise."

"Why are you doing this, Brennan? You're treating me like a stranger."

"I'm not doing anything, Elle. I just happen to be a very busy man right now. Surely you can understand that?"

She stiffened. "Yes." Elle ran a trembling hand through her hair. "Well, I'm sorry to have bothered you. I'll leave you to your work."

"Elle . . ."

Waving her hand in dismissal, she responded, "Good-bye, Brennan."

By the time Elle made it to the car, she couldn't stop her tears from flowing. What was happening to them? Why was Brennan trying to push her away?

By the end of the week, Elle was bone-tired. All she wanted to do was catch up on her reading and watch some television.

The doorbell sounded, adding to her irritation. Brennan was still acting strange and distant. He and Malcolm were out playing golf. At the moment she didn't feel like company.

Before she reached the door, the doorbell rang a third time. "I'm coming," Elle snapped. "Just give me a minute."

As soon as she glimpsed her visitor, Elle wanted to slam the door shut.

"Is Brennan here?" Charis demanded.

"No, he's not."

"Are you sure?"

Elle fought to keep her temper in check. "Yes, I'm sure. Look, I'm not in the mood for you or your attitude. . . ."

"You're the one with the attitude."

"Good-bye, Charis." Elle started to close the door.

Sticking her foot in the doorway, Charis called out, "Wait!"

"*What is it?*"

Charis asked, "Did you and Brennan have a fight?" She stepped around Elle.

"I'm sorry to disappoint you, but no, we didn't."

"You look a little sad. Are you sure everything's okay between you two?"

"We're fine, Charis," Elle replied.

"I'm sorry you got caught in the middle of this situation. However, you could have avoided all of this mess if—"

"If I hadn't married Brennan," Elle finished for her. Her arms folded across her chest, she rolled her eyes heavenward. "Why can't you get this straight? Brennan asked *me* to marry him. He didn't *want* to marry you." She immediately felt guilty over her outburst. Sighing heavily, Elle replied, "This is a difficult situation for all of us."

"You could have walked away," Charis pointed out.

Elle almost felt sorry for the woman. "If you'd told him about the baby sooner, maybe things would've turned out differently for you. Why did you wait until you found out he was getting married?"

Charis pointedly ignored Elle's questions. "He doesn't love you. He was extremely angry because I didn't tell him about Lauren. Marrying you was his way of hurting me."

"I think this conversation is going nowhere." Gesturing toward the door, Elle announced coldly, "It's time for you to leave."

"I'm only trying to spare you some heartache. Brennan will never love you."

Elle lost her temper then. Everything she felt about Charis rose to the surface. "Who do you think you're fooling? You don't care a fig about me or my feelings. If you did, you'd stay out of mine and Brennan's life. *Why don't you and your child go back to Hawaii?* Then Brennan and I can finally have the life we deserve."

"That's enough, Elle," a deep bass voice ordered.

Startled, Elle glanced over her shoulder and saw Brennan standing there. She hadn't heard him enter the house. He must have come through the garage, she surmised. She could almost feel his wrath when he moved to stand beside her.

"Charis, could you please leave the room?" he asked. "I need to talk to my wife."

Giving him a sexy smile, she replied, "No problem. I'll be in the den."

As soon as Charis walked away, Brennan turned to face his wife. Careful to keep his voice low, he demanded, "Where do you get off telling Charis that she and Lauren should stay out of our lives? That's my daughter you're talking about. You have no right."

Elle could hardly believe her ears. "Excuse me?"

A warning cloud settled over his features. "You heard me, Elle. Charis is Lauren's mother. Like it or not, they are a part of our lives and always will be."

Elle frowned with cold fury. "Believe me, I'm well aware of that. Instead of reminding me, why don't you explain to her that I am the one you married. *Or have you forgotten that as well?*" Tears welled up in her eyes. "I'm so tired of you and Charis!"

"Honey . . ." Brennan reached for her, but Elle retreated a step, saying, "Just leave me alone."

"I don't want to fight about this, Elle."

She stared at him in disbelief.

Trying to calm her, Brennan said, "Look, I know this is a difficult situation for all of us, but I'm trying to do the best I can."

Wiping her tears away, Elle said, "I realize that, Brennan. But you have to know that Charis and I are never going to be friends. I don't trust the woman."

"Just because she and I have a daughter, you don't have to feel threatened."

"Oh, please. It's not like that, Brennan. I'm not insecure. I just don't trust her and I doubt I ever will."

Brennan pulled her into his arms. "Will you at least make an attempt to get along with her? Believe me, I know Charis is a piece of work."

This time Elle did not pull away. "I can't make any promises. I won't be disrespected in my own home any longer. She comes over here and acts as if this is her house. If she had her way, I wouldn't be here."

"You know that this is your home. Mine and yours, so why do you let her get to you?"

"Let's just drop it, Brennan. You don't understand."

"I'm trying," he shot back.

"Forget it." Elle glanced over at the clock. "It's getting late. Charis should get home to her daughter."

"You're not going to let up, are you?"

Elle opened her mouth to speak, then closed it. Shaking her head in frustration, she rushed out of the room. She found Charis lurking in the hallway, a silly grin on her face.

As much as she wanted to slap the woman, Elle decided to ignore Charis instead. She heard Brennan calling out to her, but Elle just kept on walking.

They would never see eye to eye when it came to Charis Wentworth.

Elle was already in bed when Brennan entered their master suite. He kept his eyes on her while unbuttoning his shirt.

She kept her eyes glued to the book she'd been reading and refused to even acknowledge him until he spoke to her. Even then Elle looked at him with defiance.

"What did you say?"

Brennan repeated his words. "I'm worried about you. Are you feeling okay?" She seemed so emotional these days.

"I'm fine," Elle replied coldly before returning her eyes to her book.

Brennan sat down beside her and took the novel from her. "I don't believe you. Lately you haven't seemed happy. I know something's wrong." He took her hand in his. "Is it because you haven't gotten pregnant yet?"

Elle tried to snatch it away, but Brennan held on. "Sweetheart, don't act like this. We need to get this all out in the open, so tell me what's bothering you."

"What for? It's not like you're going to do anything about it. Besides, you're a fine one to talk. You refuse to open up to me. When you do, you take off and run like a scared little boy."

He didn't miss the bitterness in her voice. Softly stroking the back of her hand, Brennan gave her a gentle smile. "I'm listening, Elle. As for running away . . . well, maybe I have been doing that. I'll work on it."

She gave a sad sigh. "I have to be very honest with you. I don't like Charis. I've tried, Brennan. I really have."

He ran his fingers the length of her thigh. "She upsets you that much?"

"Do you know that she was in the hallway listening to us earlier? I'm telling you, the woman has no morals whatsoever and she's sneaky. Not to mention she's very disrespectful and she goes out of the way to make me feel like an outsider."

"I'm sorry."

Elle seemed a little taken aback by his apology. "For what?"

"I'm sorry for bringing all this baggage into our marriage."

"Your little girl is not baggage. She is as much a victim in all this as you are. I think Lauren's adorable and she's a part of our family."

"Do you mean that?"

"Yes, of course." Elle gave him a bright smile. "I wish . . . I'll do my best to get along with Charis."

"Thank you, sweetheart." Brennan kissed her in gratitude.

Elle had been so right about his running away. The truth was that he was tired of running, but he was scared. Something Charis had told him right after their breakup resurfaced. If his own parents didn't love him, how could he expect anyone else to love him?

Of course, she'd later tried to recant the hurtful remark, but the damage had been done. Pushing away the very thought that had defined his future for him, Brennan sought his wife's attention. Only Elle could lessen the pain he'd come to live with.

Elle could sense Brennan's need for her. With all her heart she wanted to love him and have him return that love. How could she heal his wounded spirit?

Looking over at him, Elle knew by the look on Brennan's face that he was thinking of her anatomy now. She was soon trapped by his tantalizing warmth, his arms enveloping her. Primal yearnings surged through her as she teased her tongue against Brennan's mouth.

He groaned and held her tightly. His hands roamed across her shoulders, her back, down her waist and beyond, causing Elle to moan in pleasure.

Through a fog of thickening desire, Brennan and Elle made love.

Elle woke up in the middle of the night sometime later. She turned over expecting to find a sleeping Brennan lying beside her, but the space was empty. He was gone.

Crawling out of bed, Elle eased into her robe. She stuck her feet in soft slippers and headed to the door. She took the stairs slowly and walked straight to the library. Brennan wasn't in there. Next, Elle checked the media room, and it was empty as well.

She ventured throughout the house, but still no sign of Brennan. Elle held back her panic. Surely he would come back. He wouldn't leave her again.

Chapter Nineteen

Brennan needed a clear head, so he decided to take a walk on the grounds of his estate. He ended up in the rose garden. Elle loved roses, and now he realized that he'd had her in mind when he'd had the colorful assortment of roses planted there.

Every time he looked at his wife, Brennan felt a surge of happiness. It was an emotion unfamiliar to him. But that wasn't the whole of it, either. He could no longer deny the truth. He was falling in love with Elle.

Brennan was afraid to just let go with his feelings. The feelings of rejection and the painful memories of his childhood would not dissipate, so he kept his heart constantly guarded. He didn't want to endure any more heartache.

Brennan felt a small hand on his shoulder, and he quickly turned to see who it was. Brennan relaxed at seeing his wife. "What are you doing up?"

Elle pulled her robe tighter. "Looking for you." She sat down on the bench beside him. "Can't you sleep?"

He shook his head. "Not really."

"Brennan, is there something on your mind? I gave you my word. I *will* try and get along with Charis."

"It's nothing like that, sweetheart." He slipped an arm around her. "You should be sleeping."

"I don't sleep well when you're not there. It's because of the night you left—" Elle paused then added, "I'm sorry. I'm not trying to make you feel bad or anything."

"I understand. Honey, I am very sorry about the way I handled that situation. I promise you I will never ever leave you like that again. Please trust me on that."

"Will you come to bed then?"

Brennan knew, without a doubt, he loved this woman sitting here with him. He could not see his life without her. Although he couldn't say the words, Brennan decided to show her as best he could.

Rose petals were strewn throughout the house the next day, marking a path to the master bedroom. Brennan grinned as he followed the trail.

The bedroom had been transformed into a tropical paradise. Plants and exotic flowers had been placed all over the room. A small table containing chilled shrimp, lobster salad, strawberries, and an assortment of other goodies had been brought up to the room.

Elle was dressed in a long strapless dress with a high slit bearing her leg. Brennan inhaled the fragrance she wore. It was the new Advantage cologne. Warmth flowing through him, he murmured, "You look so exquisite."

Elle smiled shyly.

He glanced around the room. "What did I do to deserve all this?"

"I went to the doctor today."

"Oh." Comprehension dawned. Brennan started to grin.

"I'm not pregnant yet," Elle announced quickly. "But he said that I'm as healthy as a horse. There shouldn't be any reason why we can't have another baby. That is, if you still want one. Do you?"

Brennan reached for her in response.

"Hello, darling," Charis cooed in Randall's ear as she brushed by him and into his condo.

"What are you doing here?" he questioned. "I don't recall inviting you here."

Raising fine, arched eyebrows, Charis protested, "Surely you don't want me to leave? This is something you've wanted for a long time." Pushing him back onto the sofa, she bent down low enough to give him a close-up view of her full breasts.

Randall kept his eyes trained on her face. "Not any-more."

"Even if I tell you I'm ready?" she questioned. Charis eased down on his lap. Stroking his chest, she stated, "I want to get married one day and have more children. It's the same thing you want, isn't it?"

"I asked you a question, Charis. Why did you come here?"

She smiled suggestively. "I wanted to spend some time with you. I was lonely."

Randall moved so that Charis had no choice but to sit down on the couch. He rose quickly and strode over to the entertainment unit. Picking up his car keys, he announced, "You're going to have to visit somebody else. I've got plans. Next time pick up the phone and call first."

Charis shot to her feet. "I didn't realize you were so mean." Pouting, she muttered, "I don't know what I was thinking about. Wanting to marry you."

"Charis, I'm flattered, but I'm not interested. You're going to have to find yourself another fool."

Her back went stiff and anger flashed in her eyes. "What is your problem?"

"I don't have a problem, Charis. You do. The only reason you're here is because you can't have the man you really want."

She headed to the door. "Think what you'd like, Randall."

When the doorbell rang, Elle's body tensed. She knew it was Charis, because she was bringing Lauren to the house. It was Brennan's weekend with his daughter.

"Brennan called from the car. He should be here shortly," Elle announced. "Lauren and I will have a little playtime until he gets here."

"Oh, no. I'm staying here until he gets home."

Catching herself, Elle held back her retort. Charis opened her mouth to speak, then changed her mind. She made herself at home on a nearby chair. Lauren played at her feet.

Elle watched the toddler, a smile on her face.

"She looks just like Brennan, don't you think?"

"So does Randall," Elle commented coolly. "As a matter of fact, seeing how close you and Randall are . . . well, either man could have fathered her."

"How dare you!"

"What's wrong, Charis? Did I strike a nerve?" Laughing, Elle walked out of the room. She was pretty sure that Charis had something to hide. But how could she broach the subject with Brennan? He loved Lauren, and losing her could devastate him. Nonetheless, he deserved to know the truth. She vowed to find out exactly what that truth was.

Chapter Twenty

"What have you been telling that little mouse?" Charis railed.

Randall put aside the proposal he'd been reading. "I don't know what you're screeching about."

"Elle practically accused me of lying about Lauren's paternity."

There was a thin smile on his lips. "Really? Now, that's very interesting."

"Perhaps you'll find this just as interesting. Elle thinks it's *you* who fathered my child. Perhaps now you'll wipe that amused expression off your face."

Shocked, Randall shot up straight in his chair. "What?"

"She thinks you're Lauren's father."

His dark eyes widened as the reality of what she'd said sank in. "But you and I never slept together."

"I know that, but Elle doesn't."

"How in the world did she come to that conclusion then?"

Shrugging, Charis stated, "I think she's just reaching for the moon. She hates the fact that Brennan and I are becoming closer and closer."

"I think you're reaching for the moon on this one," he muttered. "My cousin is with the woman he wants."

"For now. Next week, next month, or even next year might be a different story."

"Give it up, Charis."

"Actually, I've been thinking along those lines."

Randall frowned in disbelief. "Since when?"

"You know, I've been thinking about you."

"Really?"

"A lot, actually. I think we could have been good together."

"I don't think I have enough money for you. That is the reason you chose Brennan over me, isn't it?"

Charis pretended to be offended. "I have my own money."

"No, you don't. When your father died, he left you and your mother with nothing but a lot of debt. It's only by the kindness of your father's attorney that your mother was able to keep the house. Even I'm curious as to how she's been able to maintain a full staff of servants and her lifestyle."

"I still have my trust fund. I've been taking care of everything." Charis saw no need to inform Randall that Elizabeth Cunningham was her benefactor, and now Brennan was being very generous.

"Which has to be getting smaller and smaller as we speak. You may want to think about getting a job."

"You're crude. Brennan has seen to it that Lauren and I are provided for." She eased onto his lap. "Now, back to us. Why don't I meet you back at your place?"

"I don't think it's a good idea. I would think you've had enough of my family."

"You can be so cruel when you want to be. I don't like that about you." Having said that, Charis stormed off. She was furious. Nothing was going as planned. Charis realized that if she wasn't careful, she could lose everything. She would have to pull out all the stops.

Jordan and Elle met for lunch. As soon as they were seated, Jordan asked her, "How are things going?"

"Okay." Picking up her menu, Elle tried to decide on what to order.

"Charis isn't getting to you, is she?"

"No, not really." She turned to face Jordan. "How well do you know Charis?"

"I don't know her well at all. I just get these strange vibes whenever she's around. I don't trust her."

The waitress arrived to take their drink orders. Both women ordered water.

Leaning forward, Elle inquired, "Do you know if she's ever had anything going on with Randall?"

Jordan was clearly surprised by her question. "Not that I know of. She and Randall went to school together. In fact, he's the one who introduced her to Brennan."

The waitress returned with their water. She took their food orders. When she disappeared into the crowd, Jordan turned her attention back to Elle. "Why would you ask something like that?"

"I was curious, that's all. I noticed they seem pretty close."

"You think Lauren is really my brother's baby?"

Elle met Jordan's gaze. "I thought there might be a possibility."

"Don't you mean you hope so?" Jordan smiled. "I hate to disappoint you, Elle, but I think you're way off base on this one."

Elle refused to let the subject drop. Her intuition was going into overdrive. "I still think there's something going on between the two of them."

"Well, if Randall was Lauren's father, he would let it be known."

"Only if he had knowledge of the fact," Elle countered. "I'm telling you—your brother knows more about this situation than any of us."

Frowning, Jordan shook her head. "I don't think so. Randall's not like that. If he knew something, he would tell it."

Elle played with her water glass. "Even if it meant hurting Brennan?"

Jordan didn't respond.

Their food arrived, and while they ate, Elle decided to let the matter drop.

Charis hung up the phone after her call from Randall. He was furious after his sister's recent visit. She smiled. So, Elle had gone to Jordan with her suspicions. It didn't bother Charis, because she had a plan. It was time to make her next move.

A few hours later, she stormed into Brennan's office, despite his secretary's loud protests.

He looked up from his monitor. "Charis, what are you doing here? Is something wrong with Lauren?"

"No, Lauren's fine." She pretended to wipe a tear from her eye.

"Then what is it?"

"Brennan, I hate to tell you this, but it's about Elle. Your wife is spreading vicious lies about me."

He blinked rapidly. "What are you talking about?"

"Elle's telling people that Randall and I slept together. She's saying that Randall fathered Lauren."

Brennan burst into laughter.

"What are you laughing at? This is certainly no joke."

"Elle wouldn't say anything like that. How would she know whether or not you and Randall would sleep together?"

"Call Jordan. She'll tell you."

"This is so ridiculous."

"You won't think so after you hear what Jordan has to say." She grabbed her purse and headed to the door. "You wife is getting desperate, Brennan. It's a shame she's so insecure."

When Charis left, Brennan picked up the phone and dialed Jordan's private line.

When Brennan arrived home, he found a note from Elle saying she was having dinner with Jillian and Regis. He fixed himself a drink and prepared to wait. He and Elle needed to have a talk about her obsession with Charis.

Elle arrived home an hour later.

Brennan confronted her as soon as she walked into their bedroom. "Elle, have you lost your mind? Where do you get off accusing Randall and Charis of having an affair?"

"Who told you that?"

"Charis came to see me and she was very upset. I have to admit that I can understand why."

"You're defending her?" Elle was furious. "I can't believe you can't see it for yourself. Charis is hiding something."

"What?"

"I don't know, but I intend to find out."

"Why don't you just leave it alone? I'm married to you, Elle. Isn't that enough?" he shouted.

"This isn't about jealousy, Brennan," she shouted back. "You think entirely too much of yourself. *This* is all about the witch you've allowed into our lives."

"Elle, get a hold of yourself. I really have no tolerance for childish antics. I'm too old for that."

She shoved him as hard as she could. "I'm sick and tired of you calling me childish. I'm a grown woman, and I'm not going to sit back and let some other woman run my house."

Brennan gripped her by the arms. "Why can't you be more rational? It's not her fault that our son died, or that we haven't been able to conceive."

His words wounded Elle. "How can you say that?"

"I'm sorry, sweetheart. I'm just tired of being drawn into the battle between you two."

"You got us into this mess, Brennan," she shot back. "It wasn't me." Tears slipped from her eyes. "You should have married Charis—then you could all be one happy family."

"Stop being dramatic, Elle. I didn't want to marry her."

Her voice was low and she sounded sad. "I can't take this, Brennan. All of our fights are either about Charis or my family. Can't you see something's wrong?"

"What are you saying to me?"

"I don't think our marriage is going to work. We can't go on like this."

"You're ready to give up on our marriage?"

"No. I'm tired of trying to maintain a marriage all by myself. You're certainly not working with me on this. You want all the benefits of marriage but without love and commitment." She put a hand to her face to stop her crying. "All I want is a normal marriage. Not a facade of one. I deserve better than that."

"You agreed to this marriage, Elle."

"I know, but I can't do this. I can't."

Elle strolled over to her closet and pulled out a suitcase.

"Where are you going?" Brennan asked.

Hugging her middle, Elle looked him straight in the eye. "I'm going to my mother's house."

"Why?"

"I need to get away from you and this house. I need to think."

"This is crazy, Elle."

"Whatever," she shot back. Pulling a handful of clothing out of the closet, she stated, "Right now I don't care. I just want to get out of here."

"When will you be back?"

Throwing the clothes into the suitcase, she shrugged. "I don't know."

The next sound she heard was the door closing as Brennan left the room. Anguish tore at her and Elle drew upon an untapped strength to keep her nerves under control. Her hurt was too raw for rational reactions, Elle surmised silently.

Like Ivy's, her marriage was falling apart and she was helpless to stop it from happening.

Chapter Twenty-one

"Would you like some breakfast, dear?" Amanda asked.

Elle shook her head. "No, thank you, Mama. I'm not hungry."

"How did you sleep?"

"Not well at all. I talked to Ivy last night and she told me about the divorce. I spent most of the night trying to console her."

"Why didn't you wake me?"

"Mama, you need your rest, too. We were fine. We cried, cursed men in general, and vowed to stay as far away from them as possible."

"Do you want to talk?"

She nodded. "Mama, what am I doing wrong? I try not to let Charis get under my skin, but she always manages to do so. Then Brennan blames me. When I want to spend time with my family, he gets upset about that, too."

Amanda looked surprised. "He doesn't want you to spend time with us?"

"What I meant to say is that he thinks I spend too much time out here with you or the rest of the family, and not enough time with him."

"What do you think?"

"I think he's wrong."

Amanda gave a small laugh. "Yes, I suppose you would feel that way." She embraced her daughter. "Come here, baby girl. Mama's going to give you her opinion."

Elle laid her head on her mother's breast.

"I think you should consider what Brennan's saying. First of all, you are always complaining about not being able to come out as much as you'd like. And when you do come with your husband—you leave him and run off to talk to us, leaving him alone."

"That's his fault."

"You have a husband now. You have to learn to compromise, Elle."

"I thought I was."

"Maybe not enough for Brennan. Honey, if he wants you home with him—do it. Spend quality time with your husband. The way he probably views this situation, you're putting us before him. You can't do that, baby."

"I don't want to choose between you all."

"That's not what he's asking, Elle. Your husband wants the same thing you want. He wants to feel as if he comes first in your life. You want to be first in his, right?"

Elle nodded. "I feel like he puts Charis before me."

"Have you told him that?"

She shook her head. "No. We usually end up arguing and it never goes anywhere after that. There are times I wish Charis would just disappear."

"That's not going to happen, dear."

"I know that, Mama. Right now, Brennan's mad at me because I suspect that Lauren isn't his and I mentioned it to one of his cousins. He won't even entertain the idea."

"Why would you think that? The baby looks as if he spit her out. Honey, it sounds like you're reaching for the stars."

"Mama, I believe there's something Charis is hiding and it has to do with Lauren. I know it like I know my own mind."

"Elle, you have to have some faith in your husband. You have to trust that he wants a life with you. After all, he married you." Amanda paused. "Your father and I went through a bad patch early on in our marriage. We even separated for a time. I was pregnant with Preston."

"Really? You and Daddy?"

Amanda nodded. "I was never one to just give up without a fight, so I hung in there. You see, I wasn't about to give up my husband."

"Was there another woman involved?"

"For a time. But that's not something we should be talking about right now. We need to concentrate on you. Do you love your husband, Elle?"

"With all my heart," she answered.

"Then don't give him away. Fight for him."

Brennan heard the high-pitched squeal of girlish laughter. Lauren was running toward him with arms outstretched. Charis followed close behind.

"Lauren and I came by to cheer you up."

"I don't need cheering up," Brennan shot back. "I'm fine."

"No, you're not," she countered. "Your mother told me about Elle walking out on you. I have to tell you that I'm not that surprised, though."

He didn't feel like company right now. "Charis, please go home."

"You don't want to spend time with your little girl?"

Glaring at her, Brennan gritted his teeth. "I didn't say that."

He picked up the little girl. "Come here, sweetness." Brennan cuddled his daughter in his arms.

Lauren pressed her mouth to his cheek.

Charis clapped her hands with glee. "She's giving you a kiss."

"I love you so much, pretty girl," Brennan murmured. Smiling, he nodded. "Yes, I do." For a moment, he allowed himself to think of Elle.

He missed her so much, but Brennan wasn't going to go running after her. Elle would have to come home on her own. He refused to beg ever again.

"Brennan, are you okay?" Charis asked.

He nodded. He held on to Lauren as if she were his lifeline. Brennan consoled himself with the fact that at least he had his daughter.

Brennan paid little attention to what Charis was saying. He found it hard to keep his mind off of Elle and how much her absence bothered him.

"She's not worth it, Brennan."

"What?"

"Elle isn't worth mourning over. She wasn't right for you."

"How would you know?" His voice was heavy with bitterness.

Charis sighed softly. "Brennan, I'm sorry for hurting you. I was angry—"

He cut her off by saying, "It doesn't matter."

Lauren had fallen asleep in his arms, so Brennan gently laid her down on the sofa. "You should take her home. This chair isn't too comfortable, I'm sure."

"I really don't want to wake Lauren by taking her out into the night air. I was thinking we should put her in her room upstairs."

"You mean she's going to stay here?"

"Do you have a problem with that?"

Brennan shook his head. "Lauren's welcome here anytime."

"I'm not leaving her here alone. I'm staying here with Lauren."

"Excuse me? Charis, you can't stay here."

"Why not? Lord knows you have more than enough room. I'll sleep in one of the guest rooms. The one closest to Lauren's room. You have enough going on in your personal life. Let me stay and tend to Lauren."

"I don't know about this."

Charis looked offended. "I'm not going to attack you, Brennan."

"I'm sorry. It's not what I was trying to imply."

"Then let me stay. If Lauren wakes up in the middle of the night, I'll get up with her. I think a good night's sleep would do you a world of good."

"Fine, you can stay," Brennan agreed. It would be good having Lauren there, he decided. Maybe the house wouldn't seem so empty.

Charis had the unmitigated gall to burst into his room the next morning wearing a robe that hid nothing at all. Brennan hurriedly pulled the covers over his own nude body. "What are you doing in here?" he roared.

"I can't stand seeing you look so lost. All night long I kept thinking of you and how good we were together." She licked her lips seductively. "Do you remember all the things we used to do?"

"Charis, I think you should go back to your own room. I'll meet you downstairs in an hour for breakfast. We can talk then."

"I know how to make you forget all about Elle." Charis opened her robe and let it glide to the floor.

Brennan dropped his head. "Put your clothes on, please."

"This time we're going to do things my way. You need me and it's time you realize that fact. In a few minutes, I'm going to make you forget you ever heard of Elle Ransom."

"I doubt that," he muttered, the disbelief evident in his voice.

Wordlessly, Charis moved closer to the bed and crawled in. She snatched the covers off him.

"What are you doing?"

"Something I should have done a long time ago."

Elle hummed as she pulled into the driveway of her home. The early morning traffic had been steady but light, making it an enjoyable ride to Malibu.

There was much she and Brennan needed to discuss, but after the conversation with her mother, Elle felt encouraged. Their marriage still had a fighting chance.

The house was silent, and Elle's initial assumption was that Brennan was still asleep. She smiled as she crept up the curving staircase. She wanted to surprise him.

Elle opened the double doors to her bedroom. Her eyes opened wide with surprise. In the middle of the bed lay a very naked Brennan with an equally nude Charis on top of him. Shock filtered through her, reaching all the way to her soul.

She couldn't utter a word. Pain slashed through her, followed by hurt and fury. *Brennan and Charis* . . . Elle tried to will her body to move.

She must have made a sound or something, because Brennan saw her then. Muttering a curse, he practically threw Charis off him in his haste to scramble out of bed.

"E-Elle . . ."

Hearing Brennan call her by name gave her the motivation to move. Elle turned on her heel and ran as fast as she could. Blinded by tears, she missed a step and felt herself falling. She screamed.

The last sound she heard was the sickening thud of her body as she tumbled down the stairs. Elle felt her body bounce off the wooden floorboards.

She fought with all her strength to stay conscious, but along with the pain, darkness came and overtook her.

Horrified, Brennan watched helplessly as Elle landed hard at the bottom of the stairs. He ran, taking the stairs two at a time until he reached her still body.

Panic soared through him as he checked for a pulse. She was still breathing. Brennan called out her name.

There was no response.

He heard Charis's voice in the distance, but Brennan didn't have a clue what she was saying. All he cared about was Elle.

"Open your eyes, baby," he pleaded. "Please open your eyes."

Elle was still unconscious.

Charis appeared at his side. "I've called the paramedics. They should be here any minute." She tried to hold his hand, but Brennan pushed her away. Taking one of Elle's hands in his, he continued to talk to her.

"Honey, wake up. Please, God, let her wake up." He was worried about possible neck or spinal injuries. What if she was paralyzed? The thought drew him into a panic.

"She's going to be all right, Brennan."

He glared at her. "*She'd better be.*" His voice held a silent threat.

The paramedics arrived minutes later, but to Brennan, it seemed liked hours. Charis handed him pants, a shirt, a pair of socks, and his shoes.

"You should put these on."

Brennan dressed quickly, oblivious to the curious glances he was receiving from the paramedics. Right now, his sole attention was devoted to Elle.

Just as she was placed on the gurney, Elle finally opened her eyes. She grimaced and Brennan knew she was in pain. She glanced at him briefly as she was taken out to the ambulance, then closed her eyes.

She didn't even want to look at him. That didn't stop Brennan, though. He ran outside and jumped into the ambulance. "I'm going with her. She's my wife."

Guilt raged through him as he stared down at his wife. Elle looked so helpless. Every now and then she would moan softly.

"We're almost to the hospital," he whispered.

She turned away from him.

At the hospital, Brennan paced while he waited for some word from the doctor.

Charis came up behind him. "I got here as fast as I could. Honey, why don't you sit down? Pacing is not going to help."

Turning, he scowled at Charis. "None of this would have happened if you hadn't been there."

"I stayed overnight at your invitation, Brennan."

"I didn't invite you into my bed," he snarled. "Besides, I didn't exactly issue an invitation to you. I was manipulated by you, as usual."

"You're worried right now, so I'm going to overlook that remark."

Brennan had already called Amanda. He knew she would contact everyone else. Jillian was the first to arrive.

She glanced from Charis to him before asking, "What happened to my sister?"

"She had an accident. Elle fell down the stairs."

"Is she okay?"

"I don't know. I haven't spoken to the doctor."

"Mama's coming with Preston. He and his family arrived yesterday."

He nodded. Brennan hadn't met Preston face-to-face, but he'd spoken with him on the telephone a few times.

Jillian confronted Charis. "What are you doing here?"

"I'm here to give Brennan support."

"Were *you* at the house when my sister arrived?"

Charis met Jillian's hostile gaze. "Yes, I was. It was an unfortunate accident."

Jillian turned around to face Brennan. "I don't know what my sister sees in you. You'd better hope upon hope that Elle's going to be okay. If she isn't—"

The doctor's appearance stopped her threat.

"How's my sister?"

They stood there in silent expectation.

After the doctor gave his prognosis, Brennan asked to see his wife.

He eased into the room, not wanting to disturb Elle

if she was sleeping. The doctor had ordered something to help her with the pain.

In the hospital bed, Elle looked no more than fifteen or sixteen. Brennan clenched his eyes shut to block out the sight of Elle's long curling tendrils tumbling around her shoulders in disarray, and the look of pain and betrayal on her face.

When Brennan opened his eyes, he found she was still watching him. He gave her a tiny smile. "The doctor says you've got a couple of bruised ribs and you're going to be sore for a few days, but for the most part, you're going to be fine."

Elle turned away from him in response.

"Please don't turn away from me. Sweetheart, I'm so sorry. I want you to know that nothing happened between Charis and me. I—"

"Get out of here," Ray demanded from the doorway. "Leave my sister alone."

Brennan glanced over his shoulder. "Elle is my wife. I have every right to be here."

They started to argue.

"S-stop . . . it," Elle moaned. "Stop."

"I'm sorry, sis. I didn't mean to upset you."

Kaitlin rushed into the room, followed by Matt. She went straight to the bed. "Honey, I'm so glad you're okay. What happened?"

Tears slipped from Elle's eyes. Brennan looked over at his wife. "I mean it," he said in a low voice. "If you want me to go, I will."

Her voice was barely above a whisper, but Brennan heard her loud and clear when she said, "Go . . ."

Brennan nodded in resignation. He turned and headed to the door.

When he stepped into the hospital corridor, Brennan was met with hostility from members of the Ransom family. He updated them on Elle's condition.

Spotting Charis, he stalked over to where she was sitting. She rose as he approached. "I'm relieved to hear that Elle will be okay."

"I could . . . I could wring that skinny neck of yours," Brennan sputtered. "Leave this hospital and don't bother coming back. I don't want you upsetting my wife."

Tears welled up in her eyes. "I realize you're upset right now, so I'm going to forgive you."

"I want you out of here now!" Brennan couldn't seem to stop yelling. He was furious with Charis.

Amanda gently touched his arm. "We are in a hospital. This is not the time or the place."

Putting his hands to his face, Brennan dropped down in a nearby chair. "Get away from me."

Grabbing Charis by the arm, Kaitlin asked, "Do you need help getting to the door?"

Jillian was immediately beside them. "You are clearly not welcome here, so leave quietly or we will throw you out—headfirst, I might add."

Charis gasped.

"You heard my sister. Make your decision quick. You'd better consider yourself lucky I'm not the one you're dealing with." Kaitlin's tone was deadly.

"*Or me,*" Jillian added. "But if anything happens to Elle, you will have the entire Ransom clan to deal with. We will eat you alive."

"Just let go of me. I can find my own way out." Charis pulled her arm away and walked off, moving as fast as she could. She only glanced back once.

Turning back around, Jillian faced Brennan. "As for you . . ."

He stood there, shoulders slumped, listening to every vulgar name his sister-in-law called him. Rightly so, he deserved it.

Chapter Twenty-two

Elle hurt from the inside out. In her mind she could not erase the vision of Brennan in bed with Charis. The painful memory had lodged itself in her brain and would not go away.

What hurt her more was the fact that she'd allowed herself to believe that Brennan loved her in return. Now she knew better. Not only did he not love her, but he didn't respect her, either.

Laine eased into the hospital room just as she wiped away her escaping tears. He leaned over and kissed her forehead. "Hey, sis."

"Hello," she mumbled.

"Oh, honey, I'm so sorry."

Swallowing the despair in her throat, Elle replied softly, "It's okay."

Laine's lips thinned with anger. "No, it isn't. It isn't okay to hurt someone like this. To break a person's heart without even a casual thought."

"I never thought Brennan would do this to me." Elle

wiped her eyes. "I loved him so much, Laine." Her eyes darkened with pain.

"I know."

"How could I have been so wrong about him?" She gulped hard, hot tears slipping down her cheeks. "I have always believed that he loved me a little bit for me—even though he would not admit it."

Regis knocked on the door. "Can I come in?"

"Sure."

"How are you feeling?"

"I hurt . . ." Elle started to cry harder. Laine held her. When Elle's tears dried, she felt achy and exhausted. Her whole body was engulfed in tides of weariness and despair, causing her to feel drained, hollow, and lifeless.

Feeling ashamed, Elle said, "I'm sorry about that miserable display of emotion."

"You have nothing to apologize for," Regis reassured her.

"Brennan doesn't deserve my tears. He doesn't deserve my love." Her eyes strayed briefly to the door. "Is he still here?" Unconsciously, she held her breath.

"He was out there when I came in," Laine answered. He glanced back at his wife. "Was he still in the corridor when you came in?"

Regis's eyes met Elle's. "Brennan's still here. He said he wasn't going to leave. He wanted to stay here just in case you changed your mind."

Deep down, Elle had known somehow that he would still be nearby.

"Would you like to see him?"

"No, Regis. As long as he stays away, I'll be fine."

"You're going to have to talk to him sooner or later,

you know," Laine stated gently. "He's not just going to disappear."

"I know." Weariness enveloped her as she tried to concentrate. Her back ached all over and her muscles screamed. Elle moaned from the pain.

"You okay, sis?"

She nodded. "I think the medication's wearing off."

Laine kissed her cheek. "Get some rest, sweetheart. We'll try and come back to see you later tonight."

Elle shifted her weight as gently as she could, and was rewarded with a sharp, knife-like pain for her efforts.

"I'll get your nurse," Regis said. She turned and rushed out of the room.

She could hear Brennan's deep voice loud and clear. He wanted to know what was going on. Elle heard Regis, her voice soothing as she assured him everything was fine.

"Would you tell Brennan to go and get something to eat?" Elle asked of her brother. "Just make him go somewhere, please."

When Laine left, Elle's mind flashed back to the fall. Lucky for her, she'd escaped with only bruised ribs. No broken bones. However, her heart hadn't been so fortunate. Her heart was broken.

Later that evening, Brennan strolled into the room carrying a dozen roses. "I know you don't want to see me, but I thought these might cheer you up."

Elle nodded once, unsure of her ability to speak.

"How are you feeling?"

"Fine," she answered without inflection.

"Honey, please talk to me."

She looked over at him. "What do you expect me to say?"

"I know you're hurt and you're angry. You have a right to be, I suppose."

"You suppose?" They stared at each other for a minute.

"I'm not trying to upset you. Right now I want you to get better."

Elle tried to move her body. She cried out in pain.

Brennan reached out to help her. "What's wrong?"

"Hurts when I move."

"I'm so sorry, honey. If I could switch places with you, I would."

She moaned softly.

"Do you want me to get a nurse?"

"No. I just need to get some rest. I feel tired."

He nodded. "The doctor is going to keep you overnight, so I'll come back in the morning."

Elle wasn't up to coping right now. "You don't have to do that. I'm sure you're busy."

"I've never been too busy for you, Elle. I'll stay here with you all night long, if that's what you want."

She shook her head. "No, don't bother."

"Why are you trying to push me away?"

Her eyes were bordered with tears. "I think you know the answer to that question. Right now, I just need time alone."

"I'm . . . I know I can't apologize enough for what happened. Elle, I do not want Charis. You are the only woman I want in my life."

"Don't, Brennan . . ." Elle shook her head sadly. "I need you to leave."

"I'm going to leave, but I will be back in the morning."

Her tear-filled gaze met his. "If you care anything at all for me, Brennan, please stay away. I can't handle seeing you right now."

"You don't mean that."

"Yes, I do," she said.

Before he left, Brennan planted a kiss on her forehead. The warmth of where he'd placed his lips remained with her throughout the night.

Brennan arrived just as Elle was given her discharge papers. "Why didn't you tell me that you were getting out of the hospital? I would've come earlier."

Elle didn't say a word.

"Did you hear me?" he prompted. He reached for her hand, but she pulled it away.

"I'm not going home with you, Brennan."

He looked stunned for a moment. "Don't do this. I'm still your husband. You belong home with me."

"You should've thought about that before you had Charis in our bed." Her voice was filled with raw pain.

"I'll explain all of that to you as soon as we get home. Elle, I miss you and I want you home where you belong."

She looked up at him. "I can't go back to that house."

He was trying to hide his panic. "Elle, I want us to discuss this at home. If you don't want to go there, then we can go somewhere else. We'll take the plane and fly up to the cottage on Torch Lake. It'll be the perfect place for you to recuperate. No one will disturb us there."

Shaking her head no, Elle stated, "I don't want to go anywhere with you. Brennan, I can't stand the sight of you right now. I just want you out of my life."

Brennan was hurt by Elle's declaration. She wanted

nothing more to do with him. She had every right to be angry with him, but Elle wasn't making it easy for him to explain anything. He had to find a way convince her to hear him out.

Brennan negotiated multimillion dollar deals on a daily basis, but he couldn't figure a way out of this mess.

Elle refused to go out to her mother's. Instead, she went back to the house she had been renting from Jillian. Two days after she'd been home, she called John and asked him to come see her.

Seated at the dining-room table, Elle stated flatly, "John, I don't want to think about this anymore. I want a divorce."

"You're still very angry, Elle."

"I have every right to be. Brennan cheated on me, and to add salt to the wound, he did it in our bed. There's no fixing that."

Shaking his head, John uttered, "I can't believe that. What was the man thinking?"

"He wasn't thinking," Jillian threw in. "At least he wasn't thinking with his head." She stuck a french fry in her mouth.

"How soon can you have the papers ready?" Elle inquired. She refused the hamburger Jillian offered her.

"I'm not sure about this, Elle. You're too angry to think rationally."

"John, I want the divorce. Brennan and I will never work out." Her eyes filled with tears. "He's the only man I've wanted to spend my life with, but if I stay with him—he'll make me crazy."

Jillian embraced her. "It's going to be okay, sis. As much as I dislike Brennan, I agree with my husband.

Put some distance behind your anger. Then decide what you want to do."

Wiping her eyes with both hands, Elle agreed. "It's not going to matter, though. My marriage to Brennan is over."

Chapter Twenty-three

Elle pushed away all thoughts of Brennan while she worked. She wouldn't allow her heartache to interfere with her work, so as soon as the doctor gave his permission, she returned to Jupiter Records.

A soft knock on her door drew her attention. It was her secretary. "Yes, Sharon?"

"These just came for you." She carried the flowers into Elle's office. "Where do you want them?"

In the trash, she thought, but she answered, "You can put them near the window. Over there."

Brennan was not going to win her over with flowers, candy, or expensive gifts. Elle simply wasn't interested.

There was no way she could ever trust him again. The phone rang, interrupting her thoughts.

"Elle Cunningham," she stated.

"It's me," Malcolm announced. "I just wanted you to know that Brennan's on his way here. He and I are meeting for lunch."

Rising, Elle grabbed her purse. "Thanks for telling

me. I think I'm going to head out myself. I don't want to be here when he arrives. I can't deal with Brennan right now."

"I tried to convince him to meet me at the restaurant, but he refused. He insisted on coming here."

"It's okay." Elle heaved a sigh of relief when she walked out into the afternoon air. She'd made it.

"Hello, Elle."

She turned around to face Brennan. "Are you following me?"

"No, I saw you leaving the building and I came out to talk to you."

"I've told you before that we have nothing to discuss. John Sanders is my lawyer, and he'll be in touch." She kept walking to her car.

"I don't want a divorce."

"*I do*," Elle lied. "We have no marriage."

"How can you say that?"

"Brennan, you married me only because I was pregnant. Not out of love. And as heartbreaking as that was, I agreed to it. I should have been honest with myself— I can't live without love." Elle's eyes filled with tears as she got into her car. "I loved you so much, Brennan, and all I ever wanted was for you to love me back. That's all."

"Honey . . ."

She shook her head. "Please, Brennan. I can't talk to you right now. It just hurts too much."

He sighed in resignation. "When can we talk?"

"I don't know. I just don't know." Elle started her car and pulled out of the parking space.

Helpless, Brennan stared after her.

* * *

During lunch, Malcolm tried to get him to eat, but he wasn't hungry.

"Give Elle some space. She loves you, but she just needs some time alone."

"I'm not going to lose her. Elle is my wife, and she's going to stay my wife."

Malcolm shook his head in regret. "I never thought I'd see the day when you and Elle ended up like this."

"I understand why she's so angry, but she won't give me a chance to explain."

"Can you explain what happened? Is it that simple?"

"I think so. Nothing happened between Charis and me. She was trying her best to seduce me, though."

"And you were totally naked? Do you sleep in the buff?"

"Sometimes. Not very often."

"Then why this particular night? Especially with that snake loose in the house."

"I was in my own house, Malcolm. I never thought Charis would . . ." Brennan's voice died and he shook his head in dismay. "This is so crazy."

"I told you a long time ago that Charis Wentworth was bad news. It's just something about that woman."

"I can't lose Elle." Frustrated, Brennan pushed away his plate. "I can't lose her," he repeated.

"Are you ready to admit it, Brennan? Can you admit that you love her?"

He nodded. "I've loved her for so long. . . ."

"You should've told her. Instead of running off to France, you should have told Elle how you felt."

"I know that now." Brennan paused. "But it's too late. She's gone."

Two weeks later, Elle left the doctor's office in a daze. She was pregnant again. How simple life had once seemed to her, and now, how complex. She walked out to her car, sad resignation mingling with the joy she could not ignore.

As soon as she reached her house, Elle called her mother. "Mama, I'm pregnant."

"How do you feel about it?"

"I'm scared. The fall and . . ." She couldn't bring herself to finish the sentence. "My timing is bad."

"When do you plan to tell Brennan?"

Shrugging, Elle replied, "I don't know. I'm not going to wait like I did before, though. Despite all that's happened between us, he deserves to know about the baby."

"I'm glad you feel that way."

"Mama, I spoke with Jillian, and she's agreed to sell the house to me. I'm going to stay here."

"I pray that you will seek the good Lord in this. Do not lean to your own understanding, Elle."

"Mama—"

"Listen to me, baby girl," Amanda interjected. "You married this man before God. Do you think you can just walk away that easily?"

"It's not easy. I never said it was. I can't be with someone who cheated on me."

"Did he?"

Elle was stunned by her mother's question. "Why are you defending him? You don't even like Brennan."

"Honey, I don't dislike your husband. I don't really know him. Brennan hasn't given us a chance to get to know him. But that's besides the point. Before you get rid of your husband—find out if you really need to."

"I love Brennan, Mama. It's not as if I *want* to divorce him. But he and I can't be happy as long as Charis is in the picture. She won't quit until she gets her claws in him."

"She can't do that unless the two of you let her, Elle. You need to remember that. You and Brennan are one—at least that's the way you should be."

In that moment, she knew her mother was right.

"The Halloween ball is in two weeks. I hope Brennan and Elle will work things out before then. I bought tickets for them to attend," Pookie announced.

"Don't count on it, dear. I think that marriage is over." Elizabeth took a sip of her coffee. "Brennan should be grateful. Elle left without a fuss."

"You're crazy," Pookie accused. "How could you not care for your son's happiness?"

"I do care. If he'd listened to me in the first place, none of this would be happening. Instead he and Charis would be happily married."

"Your son is in pain, Lizbeth. Can't you be just a little bit sympathetic?"

"Pookie, Brennan will be fine. This little snip of a girl will not break him. He's much too strong for that. In fact, I can't remember a time when Brennan's needed anyone."

Shaking her head sadly, Pookie said, "You don't know your son at all. It's a shame, too."

"You don't know what you're talking about," Elizabeth huffed.

"I live in the same house, Lizbeth. I can see with my

own eyes. You and Edward let your child be raised by a nanny.''

''*We did no such thing.*''

''What do you call it then?'' Pookie challenged. ''You stopped working when you married Edward and had your son. Then poor Brennan spent more time with the nanny than he did with his parents. I tried to be there for him, but he wanted you. *His mother.*'' Tears welled up in her eyes. ''I could never understand why God gave you a child when it was clear you only wanted one to snare Edward. But he made me barren. It just isn't fair.'' Nearly sobbing, Pookie rushed out of the room.

Chapter Twenty-four

Brennan debated whether or not to ring the doorbell. He needed to see Elle so badly that he'd risked coming to her house unannounced. Before he could make up his mind, the door opened.

"Brennan, what are you doing here?"

"I needed to see you, Elle."

She stepped off to the side so that he could come inside. "I was actually on my way to your office." Elle followed him into the living room. "I wanted to talk to you."

He waited until she sat down before taking a seat of his own. "I'm glad to hear that. If you don't mind, I'd like to go first."

"That's fine."

"Elle, first of all, I want to say that I'm glad you're doing well." Brennan's hands trembled. "Second, I have to tell you something. Something I should have told you a long time ago."

"What's that?"

"How very much I love you."

Elle's eyes widened in her surprise.

He gave a nervous chuckle. "Don't look so shocked. I thought it was kind of obvious."

"When . . . when did you first realize this?" She placed a hand on her chest. Elle kept staring at him as if she couldn't believe what she'd heard.

"I realized it the last night I was with you before I left for France."

"Is that why you walked out on me like that?"

Ashamed, Brennan nodded. "I didn't know how to handle it."

"Why are you telling me this now?"

He could hear the pain laced in her voice. "Because you have a right to know. Because I don't want to lose you, and if I have, I'm telling you because I want to win you back."

"You loved me when you married me?"

The question seemed to hang in the air for a long tense moment.

"Yes."

Elle took a deep breath. "Why didn't you tell me? Were you afraid I would hurt you?"

"No, it wasn't that. I was afraid that you would stop loving me. I figured once you got to know the real me, you . . ." Brennan couldn't finish the sentence. "When you told me about the baby, I was never so happy. I thought we had a real chance at a future together." A hot tear slipped from his left eye.

Brennan pulled out some official-looking documents, sparking Elle to ask, "What are those?"

"The prenuptial agreement. I was so desperate to keep you in my life that I . . ."

"What is it?"

He handed them to her. "Read it."

Elle did as she was told. Shock registered on her face. "You were going to take my child if we divorced."

"I didn't want to lose you or our child. I knew you would never leave if—"

"I never would have signed these papers if I'd known about this—" Elle stopped short. "You kept telling me to read them."

Brennan nodded. "I wasn't trying to trick you. It was wrong nonetheless. I never should have done this to you. When our little boy died, it tore me apart, but what hurt most was seeing how it devastated you. I saw how delighted you became at the idea of having another baby—then I saw the fear at the thought of not being able to conceive. Elle, it doesn't matter to me whether we ever have a child together. I want you. I love you so much and I want us to have a future together." He took the papers from her and started to rip them apart. "No amount of money could ever replace you in my life."

"Brennan—" Elle began.

"I never meant for Charis to come between us. I didn't have a clue of what she was capable of, either. I'm so sor—"

"I'm pregnant," she quickly interjected.

Brennan blinked rapidly. "What did you say?"

"We're going to have another baby."

In that moment of Elle's revelation, Brennan could not contain his excitement. He wanted nothing else outside of a child born of him and Elle. He vowed to love and cherish his wife and baby forever.

She was watching him. It took him a moment to realize that she hadn't said another word since her announcement. Putting his hands together in his lap, Brennan asked, "Where does this leave us?"

"Honestly, I don't know."

"I still want our marriage, Elle. Do you?"

"I won't stay married to you just because of my pregnancy. I think that's where we went wrong."

"That's not the only reason I married you," Brennan corrected. "And you didn't just marry me because of the baby. You loved me, I know you did. I loved you, too."

"So, you're saying we got married because we loved each other—only I was in the dark."

"Yes, but not exactly in those words."

"Brennan, we have some problems we need to work out. I'm willing to do that if you are."

Relief swept through him. "You're coming home then."

Elle looked down at her hands. "I want to take things slow. I can't rush back into this marriage. I'm not going to make the same mistake twice."

He nodded in understanding. "Would you mind if I call you some time? Maybe we could start dating again," Brennan suggested. "I will do whatever it takes to save my marriage."

"Come in, Jordan." Elle gestured to one of the visitor chairs in her office. "It's so good to see you."

"How are you doing?" Jordan asked.

"I'm managing," Elle replied. Playing with her hands, she added, "I miss Brennan so much. We talk almost every night, but it's not the same."

"Then why won't you go back home? He misses you, too."

"Because we still need to work some things out."

"He told me about the baby. I'm so happy for you both."

Smiling, Elle said, "Thank you. The doctor says that everything's going great. In addition to that, I've cut back on my hours, and I'm not going to travel until after the baby comes."

"This time will be different," Jordan reassured her.

"I believe that, too." Elle chewed her bottom lip. "I have to believe it."

"I really hope you and Brennan will be as close as you two used to be. You guys love each other so much."

"I know." Elle raised her gaze to meet Jordan's. "The true test is whether or not we can survive Charis Wentworth."

"It really bothers you that she shares a child with Brennan, doesn't it?"

Elle shook her head in denial. "I think Lauren is adorable, Jordan. I don't have anything against her. I just can't stand her mother."

Jordan leaned forward, placing both hands on the desk. "You can't make him choose, Elle. You do know that, don't you?"

"I don't want to. Jordan, I can't really explain it. I just want some respect. I want to come first in his life when it comes to Charis."

"Brennan loves you. He hasn't believed in love in such a long time. If he loses you, I don't know what'll happen to him. I don't know if he'll recover."

"What do you mean, he hasn't believed in love?"

"Brennan has always felt like he wasn't loved. He even tried to convince himself that he could live without it."

"He's a very loving man," Elle commented.

"He is. His self-worth is nonexistent, though. Thanks

to dear old Aunt Elizabeth and Uncle Edward. They never spent any time with him.''

For the rest of the day, Jordan's words haunted Elle. Tearing Brennan apart was the last thing in the world she wanted. She wanted to see him whole and happy.

His happiness was her happiness. Her needs were nothing compared to his. Brennan's biggest need was someone to love. He had such a loving and giving nature, Elle believed he would shrivel up and die without someone to whom he could give his heart.

She had to wonder if she had the strength to slip back into her role as Brennan's wife after all that had happened. Elle loved him so much. *Isn't he worth fighting for?* her inner voice questioned.

The answer led Elle to leave her house and drive to Cunningham Lake Cosmetics, where she found Brennan in his office. He glanced up at her. Moving quickly around his desk, Elle placed her fingers over his lips before he could say a word. She ignored the rush of heat caused by the simple contact.

"I came here to say something, and I need to do it before I change my mind."

Brennan gazed at her in confusion.

"I'll be home when you get there tonight. Please don't be late." Elle removed her hand and kissed him on the lips. "I'll see you later."

Chapter Twenty-five

Jordan carried a bowl of popcorn into the den, scolding, "You need a woman, Randall. This place is a mess."

He burst into laughter. "Maybe I should just hire a maid."

He dropped down on the floor and reached for the remote control. "What kind of movie did you bring? Something romantic, I bet."

"Hey, it's as close to love as I'm gonna get these days." Jordan settled back on the leather sofa. "Too bad all of Elle's brothers are married. They are a nice bunch of men. Not to mention handsome as well." She tossed a handful of popcorn in her mouth.

Randall reached up into the bowl for popcorn. "Mr. Right will come soon enough. You'll probably meet him while you're out investigating a fire or something."

"What about you?" Jordan questioned. "How's your love life?"

"Nonexistent. The only person who's shown any

interest is someone I want to stay as far away from as possible.''

She laughed. ''You must be talking about Charis,'' she teased.

Randall was quiet.

Jordan leaned forward. ''Charis Wentworth is the person you're talking about?'' Putting the bowl of popcorn on the coffee table, she inquired, ''Do you want to tell me what's going on here, Randall?''

He looked up at her. ''What are you talking about?''

''You and Charis. What's going on?''

He shook his head no.

''I don't believe you, Randall. Come on, you can talk to me. Are you seeing Charis?''

''No.''

''Were you two ever lovers? Was Elle right about Lauren?''

''No.'' Randall gave a deep sigh.

''Then what is it, honey? I've known you all of our lives. There's something bothering you. What is going on between you and Charis?'' she asked a second time. ''You know it's going to eventually come out.''

Randall sighed in resignation. ''Fine, but you're not going to believe it when I tell you.''

''Try me.''

When Randall finished his tale, Jordan sat there with her mouth wide open in her shock. ''Oh, dear Lord . . .''

''I told you that you wouldn't believe it. I could hardly believe it myself.''

''I could wring Charis's neck myself. What a horrible witch. She doesn't deserve a sweet baby like Lauren.''

* * *

"Welcome home."

Brennan whirled around to find Elle standing near the doorway. He just stood there, gaping at her.

She gave him a tiny smile. "I'm glad you're home."

Grinning, he asked, "Do you call that a proper greeting?"

Elle moved to stand in front of him. She embraced Brennan and stood on tiptoe to kiss him.

"Now, that's much better," he murmured. "It feels so good to hold you in my arms again."

She stepped away from him. "Why don't you go upstairs and relax in a nice, hot bath? I'll have Robert prepare something delectable for us to eat."

"You know I couldn't get anything done after you left my office today." Brennan gave her body a raking gaze. "I kept thinking about tonight."

His lips recaptured hers. Elle's flesh prickled at Brennan's touch as she drank in his kisses. She locked herself in his embrace, enjoying the feel of his arms around her.

Reluctantly, she broke off the kiss. "I'll go run your bath. It'll only take a few minutes. Have a glass of wine and relax."

"Will you be joining me in the bath?" he asked.

Elle smiled at the vision of hope in his eyes. "I'll be back shortly."

She felt the warmth of his gaze as she ascended the curving staircase. Elle climbed with confidence, determined not to let disturbing memories run rampant in her mind.

* * *

Brennan finished off his wine. Hearing footsteps, he turned around with a lusty grin. "Sweetheart—" He stopped short. "Charis, what are you doing here?"

Frantic, Melina rushed into the room. "She just pushed past me, Mr. Cunningham. I tried . . ."

He nodded in understanding. "It's okay, Melina. I'll handle Miss Wentworth from here."

"I don't know why you keep her around." Charis pouted.

"Why are you here? Is something wrong with Lauren?"

"No, she's fine. You were on my mind, so I thought I'd better come by and check on you. You haven't seemed yourself lately."

"Charis, thank you for coming by, but it really wasn't necessary. As you can see, I'm doing fine. Now if you would leave—"

"Brennan," Charis interrupted as she took a seat. Patting the empty space beside her, she said, "Come sit down next to me. I brought over some new pictures of Lauren. You've got to see them. They are so cute."

He was quickly losing patience. The last thing he needed was for Elle to come downstairs and find Charis here. "You can leave the pictures on the table, but you've got to leave." He glanced in the direction of the stairs.

Following his gaze, Charis fumed. "Is somebody here? Do you have another woman here?"

"Yes, he does," Elle replied smoothly as she glided down the stairs. "*His wife.*"

Charis jumped to her feet. "Well, isn't this cozy? What did she do—come over here begging for you to take her back?"

Meeting Elle at the bottom of the stairs, he took her

by the hand, saying, "No, it was the other way around, actually."

Furious, Charis stammered, "You are a fool, Brennan. In fact, I'm not sure Lauren should be around you."

"Excuse me?"

"You heard me. As long as you're with Miss Thing over there, you won't see your daughter. You are going to have to choose."

Brennan looked at Charis as if she'd completely lost her mind. "This is crazy."

"You can't do this to him." Elle released his hand. "Charis, there is not a court in the country that will allow you to keep Brennan from his child."

"Who said anything about court? I will take my daughter and disappear. You'll never find us."

Elle couldn't believe what she was hearing. "Charis, you're being irrational right now."

"I mean it, Brennan. It's either me or Elle."

"I thought this was supposed to be about Lauren," Elle snapped.

Her eyes never left Brennan's face. "Lauren and I are a package deal."

"Fine." He gave a frustrated sigh. "If you want me to choose, then I will. I choose Elle. She is my wife, and I intend to make our marriage work."

Charis practically choked. "How could you choose her? How could you do this to your daughter?" Giving Elle a nasty look, she added, *"Your only child."*

"My wife never would have given me such an ultimatum. Elle knows how much I love Lauren, and she would never hurt me this way." Putting his arm around Elle, he announced, "Lauren won't be an only child. We're expecting another baby."

Charis paled.

"I love my daughter, and if you insist on running away with her, I will hunt you down like a dog, Charis. And when I find you, I'll take Lauren from you. Before I'm done with you, you won't even get visitation rights. Do not force my hand."

"This isn't over, Brennan." Turning on her heel, Charis stormed out of the room.

Elle turned to face her husband. "I would have understood if you'd chosen Charis and Lauren."

"I'm married to the only woman in the world I've ever truly loved. Now, let's go have that bath. I feel like I've just fought the biggest battle of my life."

She kissed him. "Well, it's over, honey. It's finally over."

Chapter Twenty-six

Elle and Brennan decided to host Thanksgiving dinner. She compromised by inviting Charis.

"I'm surprised you're home today. Isn't this one of those Ransom family holidays that you love so much?" Charis asked as she strolled in with Lauren.

"Yes, it is. All of my family will be here shortly. In fact, my sisters can't wait to say hello to you."

"I know how much Brennan hates being around your family. It's not fair to force him into your Cosby-like world," Charis remarked as she put Lauren down.

The toddler ran straight to Elle, who gave her a carrot stick. "Why don't you stay out of my marriage? I realize you have no life, but perhaps you could find yourself a hobby or something," Elle suggested.

"I really shouldn't complain. If you keep it up, you're going to end up losing Brennan. Once I get him, I don't intend to let him go."

"You won't get him," Elle stated flatly. "When are you going to get that through your head? For goodness sake, you've tried everything—seduction, using your own child, and what other sick games your little mind could come up with."

Charis laughed. "I've already gotten him into bed once. Only the next time, you won't be around to stop me."

Elle couldn't deny it. She hated Charis.

"If you hadn't come in the room when you did, Brennan would've been mine. He wanted me. I could tell."

Before she could stop herself, Elle slapped Charis.

Elizabeth stepped into the room. "What in the world is going on in here?" she asked.

"Charis is being her usual conniving self."

Rubbing her cheek, Charis retorted, "This crazy woman just slapped me!"

Frowning, Elizabeth confronted her daughter-in-law. "Get ahold of yourself, Elle. Charis and Brennan have a child together. You are going to have to find a way to peacefully coexist. She has just as much right to be in his life as you have." Looking Elle up and down with disdain, she added, "If not more."

Elle bit back a string of curses. She looked past her mother-in-law to find Brennan standing in the doorway. Brushing past Elizabeth, she walked over to her husband and whispered, "I've had enough of your mother and Charis. I'm going upstairs for a few minutes to calm down. I'll be back down in a while."

"I'll have a talk with them," he offered.

"Don't bother, honey. It won't do any good. Just let it go. That's what I intend to do."

Randall joined them. "Where are you going?"

She smiled. "Upstairs."

"Mother and Charis," Brennan said by way of explanation.

Randall cleared his throat. "I need to talk to you both. Do you have a moment? It's something I should have done a long time ago."

Elle and Brennan exchanged curious looks. "Sure," they answered in unison.

"What is it?" Brennan asked.

Charis was standing nearby, listening. Moving quickly, she grabbed Randall by the arm and said, "Honey, I need to talk to you for a minute."

There was an urgency in her voice. Elle heard it and she wondered if Brennan heard it, too.

"Not now." Randall pulled his arm away.

"What are you about to do?" Lowering her voice to a harsh whisper, Charis pleaded with him. "Let's go somewhere and talk before you make a grave mistake."

"The mistake is not saying something sooner."

Elle cast a puzzled look at Brennan.

"What is going on between you two?" he inquired.

"Don't do this, Randall." There was a thread of hysteria in Charis's voice now. "Please don't do this."

"I'm sorry, Charis, but I can't keep letting you hurt people. Especially my family."

By now they had a full audience. Elizabeth, Brennan's father, and Pookie had all come into the family room. Muffin and her husband followed seconds later, along with Jordan.

Looking from one to the other, Pookie asked, "What's going on in here?"

"Randall was about to tell us something, but Charis seems to want him to keep quiet," Brennan replied. "I'd like to know the reason why."

Stepping away from Charis, Randall began to speak. "There's something I should have told you a long time ago. Three years ago, while I was living in New York, I ran into Charis. Actually, that's not quite true. I sought her out.''

"Randall, don't do this," Charis pleaded. "Please . . ."

Brennan's father spoke up, surprising all of them. "She's right, Randall. There's no need to bring up past mistakes."

Ignoring them both, Randall continued. "When I found Charis, she wasn't alone. She was with Uncle Edward."

"What a disgusting lie!" Elizabeth screamed suddenly. "Why are you doing this?"

"I'm not lying. There is no need to—not on my part, anyway. Brennan, I believe that Lauren is your sister, and not your daughter, as you've been led to believe. I say this because Charis and your father . . ." Randall cleared his throat noisily. "They . . . they had been involved for a while. Even during the time you were seeing her."

Elle gasped in shock.

"You're lying!" Charis screamed.

Edward looked helplessly at his son, who said, "Well, Father, what do you have to say for yourself? Is Randall lying? He has to be lying, right?"

Elle's heart broke at the sound of desperation in Brennan's voice. He didn't want to believe his father could betray him like that.

"I . . . Charis and I . . . the two of you had had a fight one night and, eh . . . well, she was so distraught over you, son. I . . . ." He paused. "I tried to comfort her and, eh . . . it got out of hand."

"I'll say it did," Pookie threw in. "Humph! That tramp standing over there had this all planned."

"What are you saying?" Charis asked. "You think I

used the father to trap the son? Well, that's not how it was at all.''

"I don't believe you," Pookie shot back.

"I don't care what you believe. I loved Brennan once and he rejected me, so I wanted to hurt him back. Hurt him badly.''

"So you seduced his father?''

"Yes. When I found out I was pregnant, I knew Brennan would never take me back. Your mother had somehow found out about the affair, and she paid me to leave town without telling anyone about the baby.''

"Dear Lord," Elle muttered. The nightmare was getting worse. On top of that, Jillian and her family had just arrived.

"Elizabeth offered me a chance to redeem myself in her eyes. She handed me the perfect solution to my little problem, as she called it. She wanted me to pass Lauren off as your daughter instead of your sister. She thought it would keep you from marrying Elle.''

"You're despicable, Charis." Brennan's tone was filled with anger.

"Despicable is much too kind a word for her," Elle stated coldly.

"You stay out of this, you witch! If it hadn't been for you, Brennan and I would be married by now." Charis lunged for her.

Brennan pushed Elle out of the way. "You lay a hand on my wife and I'll kill you.''

The fight suddenly seemed to vanish from her. Shoulders slumped, Charis put her hands to her face, sobbing loudly.

Brennan turned to face his mother, who had been silent until now. "How could you do this to me? Do you hate me this much?''

"I don't hate you, son. I've done all the begging, the borrowing, and the stealing I'm going to do. I don't intend to start over. It was the lesser of two evils."

Elle could hardly believe what she was hearing. Face-to-face with Elizabeth, she asked, "You would step on your own son for what? To keep your marriage? Money? *What*?"

"I wasn't just going to hand over my husband to this . . . this girl."

"But she was good enough for your son," Pookie stated sadly. "Sure, we didn't have a lot of things growing up, Lizbeth, but the rags we wore were clean. The food was nothing to brag about, but it kept us alive. We have been very fortunate, I admit that, and I love this life over the one we had, but to set out and deliberately destroy family like this—no. This is not right."

"I don't expect you to understand."

"I'm so ashamed of you, Lizbeth. All these years I've always believed that, somewhere hidden, you had a heart. I see I was wrong. Elle's mother called it right on the money. You are cold. Cold and dead."

Charis reached out to Elizabeth. "I never wanted to hurt you."

Shaking with fury, she responded, "You stay away from me! You were like a daughter to me. I wanted you to marry my son. . . ." Elizabeth paused for a second. "Instead, you went after my husband."

Mustering up whatever was left of her self-respect, Charis stated coldly, "I loved Edward, and he loved me, too." Turning to him, Charis started to plead. "Tell her. Tell her how much you love me and that you wanted to leave her. Tell her, Edward."

Before he could utter a word, Elizabeth spoke up. "You listen here, little girl. You do not want to take this any further, Charis. I have fought too long and much too hard to lose what I have. Trust me. You do not want to make an enemy of me." Elizabeth's eyes turned deadly. "I will destroy you."

Her act of bravado gone, tears welled up in Charis's eyes once more. She started to cry noisily.

"Oh, shut up," Pookie snapped. "You're not going to get any sympathy here. I don't know what Brennan could have ever seen in you. Or Edward, for that matter."

At the mention of his name, Brennan walked briskly out of the room, Elle following in his wake.

Elle was crying. For Brennan.

"Elle . . ." His voice broke. He opened his arms and took a step toward her.

She flew into his arms, engulfing him. "I'm so sorry."

"Why would my father do something like this to me? Does he hate me this much?"

"Honey, are you going to be okay?"

"I'll be fine." His voice, so flat and lifeless, scared Elle. Brennan was taking this loss very hard. He wouldn't even look at her.

"I could kill Charis for what she's done to you," Elle uttered in anger.

Brennan shook his head, his brow furrowing. "Even that is too good for her."

"Son . . ."

The sound of his father's voice intensified the hurt

and the sense of abandonment he had grown up feeling. He raised his eyes to meet his father's gaze.

"I had no idea," the old man started. "I'm as much of a victim in this as you are. She . . ."

"You accept no blame in this?" Brennan asked. "You're going to put all of this mess on Charis." He shook his head in disgust. "What's done is done."

"I went to her and I questioned her about the child. She informed me that she found out about the baby after she left Los Angeles. Charis said she was already pregnant when we became . . . close."

"She lied to you both," Elle interjected.

"Look, son, I'm sorry. This never should have happened."

Brennan leaned into his wife for strength. Together, they strolled back into the living room. More of her family had arrived. The air was filled with tension. It was the worst Thanksgiving Day Elle had ever experienced, Brennan knew. It was definitely the worst for him.

"Elle and I want you and Mother to leave. We've had enough drama for one night."

His massive father seemed to shrink right before his eyes.

"Brennan, I know you're angry about this, but son, I assure you that we can get past this."

"You may be able to dismiss this at will, but I'm not like that. Father, I loved Lauren. She was my daughter. My little girl."

"I understand that—"

"No, you don't," Brennan cut him off. "You have no clue about being someone's father. Lord knows you were never one to me. When I was growing up, you never paid any attention to me. Now, as an adult, you only talk to me when it concerns the company." Squeezing Elle's hand for support, he continued.

"I will never treat my children the way you treated me. Do you know why I gave up my dreams to work with you?" Not giving his father a chance to answer, he said, "I did it to be closer to you. I thought it would . . . it would make you love me just a little bit." Brennan's voice broke.

"Business will never come before my wife and my children. I hope that you'll be a better father to Lauren than you were to me. She's a very special little girl and she deserves a lot of love."

Charis came into the room, her face tear-stained.

"Stay away from my husband," Elle warned. "You've hurt him enough." She stood in Charis's path to prevent her from coming any closer.

"This is between me and Brennan. I have to explain . . ."

"He doesn't want to hear it, Charis. You can't charm your way out of this mess. Not this time."

Charis refused to give up. "Brennan, please. If you would just give me a chance to explain."

He glared at her. "There's nothing to say."

"I love you so much," Charis cried out. "I didn't want to lose you. I panicked and it was a mistake. A big mistake. I admit that much."

"I think it's time for you to leave. Oh, and Charis . . . please stay away from us. Don't come to the house—don't even call," said Elle.

"Brennan—"

"You heard my wife," he stated coldly. "Leave our

home immediately." Brennan caught sight of Jillian and her husband gathering their things. He stopped her.

"Don't leave. I want my family to stay."

"Why are we going to see your parents again?" Elle asked. For the past four months, Brennan wouldn't even let her bring up their names—now, all of a sudden, they were in the car and on their way to see them.

Reaching over, he placed a hand on her rounded belly. "I've been thinking about everything you and your mother have been saying. It's time I talked to them. First of all, I'm going to give my father my resignation."

"Really? I know we've talked about it but I didn't realize you'd made a decision."

Brennan nodded. "I wanted to surprise you. I've been talking with Malcolm, and I'm coming on board. You're going to be seeing a whole lot more of me. Malcolm and I are going to be partners."

"That's wonderful. You love the music industry anyway. It's where you've always belonged."

"You were right, Elle. I can't choose my parents, but I can choose how I deal with them. There are some things I need to say to them in order to move on in my own life. That's the purpose of this visit."

She stroked his cheek. "I love you, Brennan. I want you to know that."

"I love you, too."

Brennan parked beside his mother's car and got out. He navigated around the car to open the door for Elle. Taking her by the hand, he led her up to the front entrance of his parents' massive house.

Smiling down at her, he said, "Here goes nothing. . . ." Brennan rang the doorbell.

Pookie met them at the door.

"How's Mother?"

"She's fine. I wouldn't worry about Lizbeth. She'll land on her feet as always."

Embracing her, Elle observed, "You're still angry with her."

"I've bought a house not too far from here. I don't even want to be around the woman. I don't think I ever knew her."

"Hello, Brennan," Elizabeth said from behind them. "Elle, how nice of you to come. I assumed this would be the last place you would set foot inside."

Elle agreed. "If it wasn't for your son, I wouldn't be here."

"She came because I asked her to. Is there a problem with that?" Brennan's gaze hardened.

"You don't have to be so defensive. I was merely saying—"

"It's not important." Brennan cut her off. "I came out here to tell you that going forward, there are going to be some changes. First of all, you will respect my wife. If not, then we will have nothing to do with you. To be totally honest, I would prefer it that way, but my loving wife doesn't happen to agree."

Elizabeth swung her eyes to Elle, then back to her son.

"Elle and I are having twins. We found out last week. We would love for you and Father to have an active role in their lives, but if you choose not—"

"No," she said quickly. "I want to have a relationship with my grandchildren."

"Again, I have my doubts about that, but Elle—she actually believes you may have some redeeming qualities."

Elizabeth cast her eyes back to Elle. "Thank you," she whispered.

"Don't thank me, Mrs. Cunningham. I pray you will be a better grandparent than you ever were a parent."

When his father joined them, Brennan told him that he was leaving Cunningham Lake Cosmetics.

Edward simply shook his head and left the room.

Elle took Brennan's hand. He glanced at her and smiled, trying to hide the sadness he surely felt. His father had abandoned him once again. But this time, Brennan was a stronger man. He had found love and a family.

A week later, Brennan Edward Cunningham II died of a massive heart attack.

After the funeral, the family went back to the house in Fremont Place. Elle tried to get Elizabeth to eat something.

"No, thank you, dear. I'm not hungry."

Elle took the plate back into the kitchen. She ran into Muffin and Pookie there.

"Lizbeth won't eat?" Pookie asked.

Elle shook her head. "She will, though, when she's ready."

"How is Brennan holding up?" Muffin inquired.

"He's doing good. There are those moments when he breaks down. When he thinks he's alone."

Muffin nodded in understanding.

"I'm going to check on my sister," Pookie announced.

Later, Elle climbed the stairs to check on Elizabeth. She overheard her and Pookie talking.

"Lizbeth, see, if you'd lost that stiff upper-crust manner you've designed for yourself—maybe your husband wouldn't have fallen into bed with that tramp.''

"Pookie, I have a terrible headache. And stop calling me Lizbeth.''

"Why? That's your name. That's what I'm talking about. You're so uptight—''

"Have you no sympathy? My husband is dead. I'm all alone now.''

"Lizbeth, it's because you won't let anyone get close to you. Remember when you and I were growing up in that tenement house? We had one room between the five of us. We didn't have any choice but to be close back then.'' Pookie gave a sad laugh. "Girl, we couldn't even afford to live in the projects.''

"What does that have to do with anything?'' Elizabeth asked stiffly.

"If it hadn't been for the good Lord above, we could still be in that same situation. Can't you at least be thankful for that?''

"I am thankful.''

"Lizbeth, I love you. What I'm telling you now is that your husband is gone. Your son is downstairs and he needs you. He loves you so much.''

Elizabeth shook her head. "Brennan hates me.''

"No, he doesn't. He wants a mother. He has always needed a mother. *You.*'' Embracing her sister, Pookie said, "Open your heart, Lizbeth. He's all you have now.''

As quietly as she could, Elle went back downstairs.

Right before she and Brennan prepared to take their leave, Elizabeth came down the stairs. She glanced nervously around the room, her eyes landing on Brennan. Tears in her eyes, she strayed over to where they were standing.

"Brennan . . .'' Her voice broke. Elizabeth placed her

lace-edged handkerchief to her mouth. When she composed herself, she started to speak again. "I love you, son. I've made some terrible mistakes and I'm sorry."

Elle embraced her husband.

"Mother, I appreciate you saying that. I really do."

"But it comes much too late. I know that you'll never forgive me."

"It's going to take some time."

Elizabeth nodded in understanding.

Pookie waved to them. "I'm going home now. I'll see you all later."

"Wait," Elizabeth called out. "I don't want you to leave, Pookie. Please stay with me tonight." Tears streamed down her face. "I would like all of you to stay here with me tonight. I can't bear being in this house all alone right now."

Brennan glanced over at his wife.

"We'll stay," Elle replied.

Pookie escorted Elizabeth back upstairs to her room while Elle and Brennan made themselves comfortable in the den.

"You are a very special woman, Elle."

She smiled at her husband. "She looked so sad, I couldn't deny her." Elle leaned into her husband and closed her eyes.

"Tired?"

Elle nodded.

"Why don't you go upstairs and take a nap?" Brennan suggested.

"No. I want to stay here with you."

"Then stretch out on the couch. You can lay your head on my lap."

Elle did as she was told. Right before she drifted off to sleep, her thoughts were of Brennan and how much she loved him. She hoped that he and his mother would finally have a real relationship.

Brennan removed his hands from Elle's eyes. "This is your surprise. I know that you never liked the other house."

"Oh, no, I loved the house—it was just too big." They were standing in the front yard of the house that Elle used to lease from Jillian.

"I have lots of vivid memories of the times we spent here," he whispered in her ear. "That's why I talked Jillian into selling the house to us."

Elle turned around in his arms. "You bought the house?"

"Yes. I thought it would make you happy."

Ray and Laine pulled up.

"What are they doing here?" Elle asked.

"We're going to play ball. Carrie told me to drop you off here and she'll pick you up after she gets Mikey."

She was pleased to see how well Brennan was getting along with her family now. He no longer stood on the sidelines or sat in corners—Brennan was one of them. Standing on tiptoe, she kissed him. "Okay. Well, I guess I'll see you later."

Ray and Laine greeted them.

"How are you doing, sis?" Laine asked. "The babies wearing you down?"

Smiling, Elle answered, "I'm tired all the time, but other than that, I'm fine."

A few minutes later, she waved as Brennan drove off with her brothers. Elle unlocked the door of her new home and stepped inside. She'd always felt safe and secure in this house, and she was thrilled that Jillian had sold it to them.

Brennan had been happy here as well. This would be the perfect place for them to begin the healing process. Here in this house, they would make wonderful and loving memories. Elle vowed to erase all of Brennan's hurts with love.

Epilogue

"This was a good idea. I'm glad we decided to come back to Torch Lake." Holding her son Daniel in her arms, Elle smiled at Brennan. "Aren't they beautiful?"

Brennan rested his eyes on Christian, who lay sleeping in his arms. "My boys are handsome."

Two months old, the twin boys were already displaying the differences in their personalities. Elle decided that Christian was more like her and Daniel was very much his father's son.

"Why don't we put these two to bed? Maybe we'll have a couple of hours alone."

A few minutes later, the babies were settled in their cribs. Elle climbed into bed, joining her husband. She snuggled closer to him.

"Mother told me that Charis and her mother moved to Texas. They have relatives there."

"Really? I'm kind of surprised Charis agreed to do something like that."

"Mother gave her a nice little settlement. She also

set up a trust fund for Lauren. Knowing my mother, it couldn't have been an easy gesture for her to make."

"It was nice of her," Elle agreed. "I'm just glad Charis is out of our lives. Lauren is always welcome, though. Maybe when enough time has passed and Charis has matured, we can ask her to let Lauren spend time with us."

"Maybe. It's not going to be for a while. Charis is a very vindictive person. More than I ever knew." Kissing Elle's forehead, he whispered, "I love you so much. You've taught me a great many things, sweetheart."

"Like what?"

"Well, family for one thing. I've come to learn that there are some families who share a bond so close that they don't need words to communicate. I've had a hole in my life for a long time. The aching just grew deeper each time I was around your family."

Elle felt his pain as if it were her own.

"Every time I witnessed you with your family, it did something to me. I was filled with envy whenever you spoke with such love and affection for every member. I used to wonder what it felt like to belong to something so solid."

"And now?"

"When I thought I'd lost you, I felt a different kind of pain. Deeper than my longing for a parent's love. This was stronger, more painful. It was my need to be the center of your life."

Elle took his hand and brought it to her lips.

"We're a family now."

Brennan nodded in agreement. Her smile took his breath away with its radiance. "I would walk away from every dime I own just to see that dazzling smile of yours."

"I guess it's a good thing you don't have to prove it."

She inched closer to him until her forehead rested on his chin.

"I would. No amount of wealth could replace love and family." Brennan held her tightly, as though he could bring her inside his skin. He kissed her, savoring her sweetness. Spending his life with Elle was all he could ever ask for. "Our legacy will be one of pride, unity, and strength. But mostly of love. Elle, my life was never complete until I met you. The first time I saw you in Malcolm's office—you made my heart sing. You, my beautiful wife, will always be the song in my heart."

Dear Readers:

I hope you have enjoyed the story of Elle Ransom and Brennan Cunningham. This is the last book in the Ransom series; however, you have not seen the last of them. Thank you so much for all of the love and support you've shown me over the past four years. It has been a pleasure bringing you stories about a wonderful and loving family along with a few of their friends.

Please continue to write and e-mail me. Your letters and words of encouragement are such a joy to read. My E-mail address is: reader@jacquelinthomas.com. I've discontinued the USA.net E-mail account, so please forward your E-mails to the above mentioned address. You can write to me at: PO Box 99374, Raleigh, NC 27624-9374. Don't forget to visit my Web site and sign up for my mailing list at: www.jacquelinthomas.com.

May God continue to pour his blessings on each and every one of you.

Jacquelin Thomas

ABOUT THE AUTHOR

Jacquelin Thomas is a multipublished author of several novels, including HIDDEN BLESSINGS, FOREVER ALWAYS, SOMEONE LIKE YOU, and LOVE'S MIRACLE. She is currently working on her next project. Jacquelin lives in North Carolina with her family.